UNCOUTH DUKE

ANNA MARKLAND

UNCOUTH DUKE
ANNA MARKLAND
THE UNDUKES BOOK 3

©Anna Markland 2023

"Manners maketh man."
~William of Wykeham 1324-1404

More Anna Markland

Anna is a USA Today bestseller who has authored more than sixty award-winning and much-loved Medieval, Viking, Highlander, Elizabethan and Regency historical romances. No matter the historical or geographic setting, many of her series recount the adventures of successive generations of one family, with emphasis on the importance of ancestry and honor. A detailed list with links can be found at https://www.annamarkland.com/

She is an an independent author, so getting the word out about her book is vital to its success. If you enjoy this book, please consider writing a review at the store where you purchased it. Reviews help other readers find books.

Uncouth Duke by Anna Markland

Book Three, The UnDukes

© 2023 Anna Markland

All rights reserved. This book is licensed for your personal enjoyment only. It may not be re-sold or given away to other people. If you would like to share this book with another person, please purchase an additional copy for each recipient. Thank you for respecting the hard work of this author. This book or parts thereof may not be reproduced in any form, stored in any retrieval system, or transmitted in any form by any means—electronic, mechanical, photocopy, recording, or otherwise—without prior written permission of the publisher, except as provided by United States of America copyright law. This is a work of fiction. Names, characters, places, and incidents either are the products of the author's imagination or are used fictitiously. Any resemblance to actual persons, living or dead, businesses, companies, events, or locales is entirely coincidental.

Cover by Dar Albert

THE GANG

DERBY, ENGLAND, 1821

Warrick Farrell stared at his father's lifeless body. "I wanted to go on hating you," he rasped, swallowing the lump in his dry throat. "All my life, I vowed to make you pay for abandoning my mother—and me, your bastard son. Then you rescued me from poverty, and I discovered I liked you."

The oak-paneled walls of Cavendish Manor's master chamber offered no reply. The physician had hurried away shortly after certifying that James Hastings, third Duke of Beaufort, had died of an apoplexy. There was no one to see Warrick's unwelcome and unexpected tears, so he let them trickle down his cheeks.

A ruckus in the hallway alerted him to the presence of his unruly wards. A sharp rap on the door soon followed. "Christ," he exclaimed, swiping at the tears with his sleeve. "That's all I need."

If he didn't let the boys in, they'd carry on bickering and probably end up pushing and shoving each other.

Black eyes and more missing teeth would be the inevitable result.

Satisfied the lighting was dim enough to hide his grief, he opened the door, a finger pressed to his lips.

Looking even more exasperated than usual, Beaufort's long serving butler had stationed his considerable bulk between the door and the orphans. "I apologize, Your Grace," Wilson intoned. "They were most insistent."

"'E's croaked, then?" Eddie Powell asked as he dodged Wilson and stepped inside.

Warrick knocked the flat cap off the lad's head. The five boys he'd brought with him when he moved from Hull had all readily agreed to dress *in proper togs* but refused to relinquish the cloth caps. They'd lived at Beaufort for six months yet still clung to this one trapping of the slums. Three tutors had come and gone, all highly recommended and experienced, but all unable to tame the lads. As a ten-year-old orphan, Warrick had survived Hull's dockland slums thanks to a kindly soul who'd taken him in. When he was old enough, he in turn sheltered street urchins who had no family. However, he was beginning to think sharing his good fortune with them had been a mistake. "Show respect," he said. "My father didn't have to agree when I asked if I could bring you lot with me to Cavendish Manor."

Hastily removing their caps, the rest of the troop filed in.

"Nice auld bloke, yon dook," Kenny Watkins whispered. "Wot'll 'appen to us now 'e's gone?"

"Reckon some toff'll teck 'is place," Tim Cooper added.

"Why's Willie callin' thee Grace?" Tom Williams asked with a snort. "Tha's nay a lass."

Warrick was quite sure he'd explained. Having long regretted that he'd cast aside his pregnant mistress, James Hastings had searched for his bastard son and named him his heir after his legitimate son's death. Apparently, the gaping gang of urchins gathered around the deathbed hadn't paid attention. "Our butler's name is Wilson, not Willie, and that *toff* would be me," he said. "I'm now the Duke of Beaufort."

Warrick might have known Charlie Hart would be the first to sneer. "Tha's 'avin' us on," he guffawed. "Is that why tha's started talkin' all posh?"

Soon, the five were rolling about on the carpet, laughing like giddy kippers.

Warrick looked back at his dead sire. "You were right, Father," he sighed. "It'll take some doing to turn this gang into respectable young men."

In truth, greater uncertainty loomed over his own future. His father had been confident a guttersnipe from the slums could become a peer of the realm. Warrick wasn't so sure. In six months, thanks to an elocution tutor, he'd rid himself of his brogue. He dressed like a gentleman and had to admit he felt good in expensive, tailored clothing. But these were outward changes. Inside, Warrick Farrell was still the wily slum denizen he'd always been.

Ushered into the drawing room of Cavendish Manor three days after receiving word of Beaufort's death, Philip Fortescue, Duke of Wentworth, was pleased to see Alex Harcourt had already arrived. "I didn't know Beaufort all that well," he admitted to his fellow duke as they shook hands. "But he and Papa were lifelong friends, so I've agreed to be a pallbearer."

"Understandable," the Duke of Harrowby replied. "Unfortunately, my physical limitations relegated me to honorary pallbearer. Let's be honest, though, we are both curious to see how Warrick Farrell is coping with his new title."

"Well, you and I have been groomed since birth to inherit and I still find the responsibilities of managing a dukedom daunting."

"Daunting is an understatement," Farrell declared as he entered the room and offered his hand. "I apologize I wasn't on hand to greet you both."

Philip and Alex exchanged a meaningful glance after shaking their colleague's hand. There was no hint of a brogue in Farrell's speech.

"You sound more like a duke than I do," Alex remarked. "How are things going otherwise?"

Farrell shrugged. "My father decided the brogue was the first thing that had to go. Not that he disapproved of it. He felt I'd never be accepted by my peers if I didn't speak like a gentleman educated at Eton and Oxford."

"Be glad you escaped Eton," Alex replied. "Philip and I helped each other survive that brutal institution."

"Right, though the slums weren't exactly an easy place to grow up. That's another thing. You use each other's given name. I just can't get used to being called Beaufort."

Philip nodded. "You'll eventually become accustomed to it, but Alex and I consider you a friend. We'll call you Warrick, with your permission."

"I'd like that and I appreciate your support. I feel rather isolated. Six months was hardly enough time to work with my father on preparing me for this. It's not something I ever wanted or aspired to."

"Whereas our births gave the two of us little choice in the matter," Alex replied. "Having your orphans here must alleviate some of the feelings of isolation."

"Actually, no. They are proving to be a trial I could do without. I'm not sure they want to leave their old life behind."

"Have you hired tutors?"

"Three have thrown up their hands in despair and left. The lads aren't the sort of pupils they were used to handling."

The men sat in silence for a few minutes, until Philip said, "I'm sure Alex agrees that we want to help you as much as possible. Thanks to you, Derrick Peploe is dead and our nemesis no longer poses a threat to our families. We're in your debt. However, short of suggesting you send the lads to Eton…"

"There has to be a better solution," Alex interrupted. "The snobs at Eton will crucify them. Perhaps a governess? Somebody like my sister-in-law."

"They wouldn't behave for the male tutors," Warrick replied.

"Sometimes, a woman can succeed where men have

failed," Alex retorted. "After you left for Derbyshire, Amelia took a position with the family of a cotton mill owner in Lancashire. Apparently, she has already tamed two hellion sons nobody could handle."

AMELIA SAXTON HAD BEEN in Warrick's thoughts constantly since he'd last seen her. When his father first introduced him to polite society, she'd been the only person who seemed comfortable carrying on a conversation with him. He'd felt like a fish out of water, but she'd put him at ease. They shared the same sense of humor and his cock stirred whenever he was near her.

A slum dweller who lived by his wits had nothing to offer a wife, so he'd never contemplated marriage. Most of the doxies in his neighborhood made a living selling their bodies. He was reasonably good looking and popular, so didn't often have to fork over hard earned coin. In return, he did little things for them. French perfume and silk hose were easy to steal from the docks. However, a fellow couldn't be too careful when it came to sexual congress. He had his occasional regulars. Clean women.

Sister to two duchesses, Amelia was far removed from that life. She smelled a lot finer than any woman of Warrick's acquaintance. Raised in a genteel family and well educated, she would be a good teacher—probably what his gang of misfits needed.

But she'd apparently secured the perfect position far away in the north. Bringing her to Cavendish Manor might not be such a good idea in any case. He couldn't deny he was attracted to her but his father had urged him to seek a wealthy heiress as his bride. Only marriage to a titled wife would establish him firmly as a member of the aristocracy. Not that he cared about acceptance, but his father had placed responsibility for the dukedom on his shoulders and given him a life of wealth and privilege—a life he couldn't have dreamt of before.

He owed it to his late benefactor to pay heed to his counsel. Besides, he was a duke now, but Amelia knew his background and likely thought him beneath her.

SERVANT OR FAMILY MEMBER?

BOLTON, LANCASHIRE

After a quick breakfast, Amelia paused outside the door of her employer's study. Her mother had constantly warned that a governess was neither servant nor member of the family. Amelia had worked for the Knowsley family for almost six months and still wasn't sure where she stood in the family's estimation. To be an educator of young people had been a lifelong ambition, so why did she feel uneasy and dissatisfied?

Mrs. Knowsley couldn't say enough good things about the changes in the behavior of Miles and Tristan. The family was wealthy and she had high hopes for her sons. The woman's aspirations of netting titled heiresses for her boys seemed all the more possible in her mind when she learned Amelia's sisters had both married dukes.

Amelia refrained from pointing out that her sisters' situations were highly unusual. While a titled gentleman might consider marrying a woman of gentle breeding and good family, few noblemen would consider betrothing their daughters to the sons of a *nouveau riche* industrialist.

Miles and Tristan's manners had improved but Amelia had attended functions as the sister of two duchesses. The rough and ready Knowsley boys would have stuck out like sore thumbs. Aristocrats could be merciless in their denigration of people they perceived as being from the *lower classes*. The fact their father was rich wouldn't help at all. They'd be ridiculed and shunned, especially since none of Amelia's efforts had succeeded in ridding them of their Lancashire brogue. The blame for that lay largely at the door of their father who was immensely proud of his Lancashire accent.

As for Mr. Knowsley himself...

In the course of Amelia's volunteer work at the home for unwed mothers established by her sister, she'd heard many stories of servants being importuned by unscrupulous employers. Mr. Knowsley's behavior toward her was always impeccable, but there was something about the glint in his eyes and his habit of winking at her that she found disturbing. Perhaps he was trying to decide if she was a servant or part of the family, or was he afflicted with an uncontrollable tic?

Now, he'd summoned her to his study. For what reason she had no idea. If he thought to make advances, she'd give her notice immediately and return to Beverley. The man she'd never stopped thinking about since she met him no longer lived in Yorkshire. Warrick Farrell had moved to Derbyshire at the behest of his father, the Duke of Beaufort. Still, she could move back into the Harrowby

Dower House with her mother—temporarily, of course, until she found another position. Having finally escaped Lady Penelope's pretentious demeanor, she wasn't anxious to endure it again. However, Eliza, Duchess of Harrowby lived only a quarter mile away. Her eldest sister was always good company, and Amelia dearly missed her nephews.

The Knowsleys wouldn't provide a character reference if she left without notice. That would make it difficult to find another post. Hoping for the best, she tapped on the door and waited for permission to enter.

Her hopes faltered when she entered the study. Smoking a cigar, her employer lounged on a settee. She'd never seen him in shirtsleeves before. It wasn't a good omen. When he patted the space next to him on the sofa, she knew she was in trouble.

"I'll remain standing, thank you, Sir," she said, praying her trembling knees didn't buckle.

"Don't be like that, Miss Amelia," he replied. "I simply want to get to know you a little better. After all, you're part of our family."

She was tempted to insist she was Miss Saxton to him, but it might be risky to beard the lion in his den. "I appreciate that, Mr. Knowsley, but..."

He moved quickly for a heavy set man, startling her as he rose from the settee and lunged for her. "Remember who pays your salary, Amelia."

Many of the unwed mothers at Winifred Oliver House had told Amelia of this same threat being used to coerce them. She tried to take a step backward, nauseated by the sickly sweetness of tobacco. When he refused to let her go, she recalled something Eliza had once taught her. Her sister thought she should be prepared if she found herself in the employ of a lecher.

When Amelia kneed him in the groin with a force born of desperation, he crumpled to the floor. "Well, Sir," she said breathlessly as he moaned, his hands on his privates. "You won't have to worry about my salary in the future. Consider this my notice. I shall leave today after I speak with Mrs. Knowsley."

"Now, don't go putting ideas in my silly wife's head," he hissed, apparently not realizing she had already opened the door. She passed Knowsley's gaping sons as she fled through the foyer.

She wouldn't reveal his lecherous behavior to Mrs. Knowsley. The scatterbrained woman would take her husband's side. But an abrupt departure would leave them all wondering and somebody might put two and two together.

BACK HOME

Amelia poured her mother a second cup of tea. It felt good to be back at the Harrowby Dower House despite Lady Penelope's constant disapproval of her daughter's decision to leave Bolton.

Fortunately, Eliza had walked from the main house to join them for elevenses.

"Perhaps you were too hasty leaving such a good position so quickly—and without notice," their mother opined yet again. "You'll not find it easy to..."

"Stop badgering my sister," Eliza interrupted. "She did the right thing."

"Dear me," their mother retorted. "Just because a man pats the seat on a sofa..."

"So," Amelia said. "What would you have done, Mama? Gone to sit next to a man in shirtsleeves with a *come hither* look in his eyes?"

Lady Penelope bristled. "Well, no, if you put it that way. I don't recall you mentioning that he had doffed his coat."

Amelia and her sister shared an exasperated glance, but there was nothing to be gained from telling their mother she hadn't paid attention. Hearing only the details she wanted to hear was her stock in trade.

"I suppose you'll have to monitor *The Times* for new opportunities," Eliza suggested.

"Yes, although it's almost a week out of date by the time Alex receives it at up at the Hall," Amelia replied.

"Plus, it's a wonder there is ink left on the pages after my husband soaks up every word."

"Well, a duke should familiarize himself with current events," Lady Penelope declared.

"It was a jest, Mama," Eliza replied dryly.

"I will apply for other positions," Amelia said, though she wasn't hopeful. "I wish there was something I could do in the meantime."

"You can be my companion," Lady Penelope said.

Amelia groaned inwardly, hoping Eliza perceived the despair in her eyes.

"Actually," Eliza said, raising Amelia's hopes. "Mildred Thompson has mentioned a need for someone to take care of her son and some of the other children at Winifred Oliver House."

Amelia's momentary optimism flagged. "But they are all infants. How old is Nicholas Thompson now?"

"Three, I think," Eliza replied.

"And something of a tearaway, I hear," Lady Penelope added.

"That doesn't bother me," Amelia said. "It's the prospect of working for *Lady* Mildred that doesn't appeal. Could I not take care of Sax and Avery for you, Eliza?"

"I would love that, and so would the boys, but there's Nanny Brown to consider. I can hardly demote such a faithful servant. And you might only be here a few weeks."

Amelia understood. "I suppose I'll speak to Mildred."

MILDRED THOMPSON WASN'T surprised Amelia Saxton had come to call. She'd heard the rumors. The girl had abruptly left a supposedly wonderful governess position in Lancashire—probably given the sack.

She really ought to be grateful to the Saxtons. The eldest sister and her husband had provided her and her illegitimate son with a place to live and a position of limited authority at Winifred Oliver House. Eliza and Alex Harcourt would have been well within their rights to leave her to fend for herself. In fact, Mildred's inability to break free of the man who had tried to kill them both could have resulted in prison, or even the noose. Derrick Peploe had shot and maimed Jenny Saxton's father-in-law, and the Duke of Wentworth died of his injuries a few months later. Yet even the middle Saxton sister seemed to bear her no ill-will.

And Amelia had always struck Mildred as a nice person.

Inwardly, Mildred knew all this to be true as she listened to Amelia's convoluted reasons for leaving her employment. Yet, she couldn't let go of the resentment she felt against the Saxtons. Two of them—commoners from an impoverished family—had become duchesses, a title Mildred could have had if she'd been able to stomach living with the disfigured and crippled Alexander Harcourt. Imagine, two nobodies were now duchesses, whereas she, the daughter of a baron was...

"Are you feeling well?" Amelia asked, jolting Mildred back to the cramped space her employers referred to as an office.

Mildred stiffened her spine. "I'm perfectly fine. You were saying?"

"Eliza mentioned you wanted to employ someone to take care of Nicholas and a few of the other children here."

"My dear Miss Saxton," she replied. "It is not I who would be the employer. The person selected would be in the employ of Winifred Oliver House. As a charity, this institution does not have the funds to pay the successful applicant. You more than anyone must be aware of that."

"I see," Amelia replied. "So, I may as well simply continue to come here as a volunteer. When I'm not teaching reading or arithmetic, I can mind the children whose mothers find employment."

"As you wish," Mildred replied. It seemed baby minding was beneath Amelia Saxton. She had just as high opinion of herself as her sisters.

"Good day to you, Mildred," her visitor said as she got up to leave.

"Good day, Miss Saxton. And it's *Lady* Mildred, if you please."

UNCOUTH DUKE

AMELIA STOPPED by Harrowby Hall before going home to the Dower House. She wasn't looking forward to being badgered by her mother on the likelihood of finding a new position.

"Mildred's just as stuck up as ever," she told Eliza.

"I know," her sister replied. "However, she did warn us that Peploe had followed when we fled to Lincolnshire. That eventually led to the wretch's demise, so I suppose we must indulge her."

"Can you believe she expects to have a baby minder free of charge? *Winifred Oliver House is a charity, don't you know, and couldn't possibly afford to pay anyone.*"

"She said that?"

"Indeed. I didn't expect to be paid, but I don't feel obliged to do anything to help that…that…"

Words failed her.

"I get the picture," Eliza said.

Mention of Derrick Peploe resurrected memories of the day the Harcourts and Saxtons had finally been freed from his threats. Amelia vividly recalled the overwhelming gratitude she'd felt when Warrick Farrell fatally shot Peploe. And he'd been quick to take action that likely saved the Duke of Wentworth's life after Peploe wounded him. She fondly remembered the part she'd played in helping him administer aid. Warrick had used his cravat to staunch the bleeding. He'd taken off his coat too. It felt wonderful to be almost touching his powerful body as they knelt together in the dirt to tend a stricken man. Of course, her mother had censured her for getting too close to a man in shirtsleeves.

The irony!

"Aunty Amelia," a bright-eyed Sax cried as he entered the drawing room and ran into her open arms.

Jolted from her reverie, she hugged her nephew and whispered close to his ear. "How I missed you, Sax."

"Did you come to play with me?" he asked.

"Of course. Where is that brother of yours?"

"Avery's sleeping. He sleeps a lot but Mama says that's what babies do. Papa bought me a puppy. He has to live in the stables. Want to see?"

"Of course. Lead on."

Sax took her hand and dragged her out of the drawing room. She resolved to enjoy her nephews while she had the chance. A new position would turn up, she was sure of it.

MURKY WATERS

No one, least of all the late Duke of Beaufort, thought he'd have so little time to prepare his newly-appointed heir for his role. Warrick and his father had spent most of the six months getting to know each other and dealing with what his father saw as priorities. Warrick had been taught to ride, how to speak the King's English properly and how to dress appropriately for different occasions.

He discovered a love of horses and thoroughly enjoyed the exhilaration of daily gallops across Beaufort's meadows with the head groom.

He had never been ashamed of his brogue, but understood the necessity to get rid of it. It was an unfortunate fact of life that a person with a working class accent was automatically deemed to be ignorant.

Learning to tie a cravat and choosing the correct attire for afternoon tea struck him as a waste of time since the valet hired by his father, a diminutive Spaniard named Carlos, had impeccable taste and made the choices for him.

Unfortunately, there'd been no time to apprise himself of things that really mattered. He'd been introduced to the estate manager but knew nothing about the dukedom's sources of income. He'd been too ashamed to tell his father he could neither read nor write and Beaufort had apparently not realized that his bastard son was illiterate.

Now, Warrick would have to navigate the murky waters of accounting ledgers and legal documents. And how was he supposed to take his seat in the House of Lords and vote on matters of national importance if he couldn't read? Sooner or later, his ignorance would become obvious and the dukedom of Beaufort would be a laughing stock. An advantageous marriage would be out of the question.

If he'd swallowed his pride and admitted he was illiterate, his father would have discretely remedied the problem. Now, he'd have to figure it out himself. There was only one person who could help him but she was employed as governess to a family in Lancashire. And he wasn't entirely sure he wanted Amelia to know his secret.

Preferring anyone's company to the constant censure of her mother, Amelia spent most of her day tutoring at Winifred Oliver House or with her sister's family at Harrowby Hall. At the latter, she was afforded an opportunity to peruse *The Times* shortly after it arrived. Unfortunately, the advertisements for governesses seemed to have dried up. Still, she enjoyed playing with Sax and his wolfhound. Judging by his huge paws, Brutus would probably grow into an intimidating beast the size of a small pony. But he was playful and obviously devoted to Sax.

Her older sisters had more or less monopolized Sax when he was a babe. Now, Amelia had the chance to watch his baby brother blossom. She became adept at changing Avery's nappies and learned how to soothe him when he fussed. She dreamt of a day when she might sing her own babe to sleep. The way things were going, she'd likely end up a crotchety old maid—a beloved aunt, but never a mother. It was enough to move a girl to tears, especially when her imaginary babe had Warrick Farrell's unmistakable green eyes and dark hair.

Relief from her growing listlessness came one day as she was eating lunch with Eliza, Alex and Sax. "I received a letter from Jenny," Eliza announced. "Our sister is expecting again."

Elated for Jenny and her husband, Amelia refused to acknowledge a twinge of jealousy. "I remember Jenny's despair when she believed Philip was lost to her. She was especially distraught when we spied on the bookshop in Hull and she thought Philip had gone there to meet Mildred."

"It all worked out in the end and now she's the Duchess of Wentworth," Alex chimed in.

Amelia sighed. "I just wish she wasn't so far away in Lincolnshire."

"Raventhorpe isn't that far," Alex replied.

Eliza agreed. "And Jenny is bemoaning the fact she's feeling exhausted while trying to complete the refurbishment of Wentworth Manor."

"Good thing she's making changes," Amelia said. "The decor in that house was awful."

"You've an eye for that kind of thing," Eliza said. "Why not spend a few weeks with Jenny? I'm sure she'd appreciate your help."

"They say a change is as good as a rest," Amelia replied. Obviously, Eliza and Alex had sensed she was drifting like a boat torn from its anchor. "Perhaps I will go to Raventhorpe, but don't let Mama know about Jenny's babe yet, otherwise she'll insist on accompanying me."

"I'll try," Eliza replied. "But she's like a bloodhound. Once she senses something's afoot, she keeps on the scent."

The prediction proved only too true. Two days later, Lady Penelope and Amelia set off for Lincolnshire in one of the Harrowby dukedom's comfortable carriages.

WARRICK PACED the confines of his father's study. It was his study now, but he couldn't yet see himself conducting business there. The three graybeards from Mawdsley, Mawdsley and Mawdsley—solicitors who had represented the interests of the dukedom for decades—eyed him nervously.

"I can assure Your Grace," William Mawdsley

drawled, peering over his pince-nez. "There is nothing untoward about the documents we have brought for you to sign."

"Just a quick signature and your seal," Josiah Mawdsley added. "In the appropriate places, of course."

Warrick eyed the beribboned portfolio on the desk. He could scarcely scrawl an X as his assent to assume the rights and responsibilities of the Beaufort dukedom. "Leave them with me, if you please," he said, ignoring the sputtering disbelief of his visitors. "A week should be sufficient for me to peruse them."

"A week, Your Grace?" Archibald Mawdsley retorted. "That's..."

Warrick held up his hand, a dismissive gesture he'd often seen his father use. He was relieved when it worked as well for him as it had for his sire. The three solicitors bowed their way out of the study.

Warrick slumped into the leather chair at the desk. "Hopefully, a week will be enough time to take advantage of Wentworth's offer of help."

Wilson's polite cough alerted him to the butler's presence. "Luncheon is served, Your Grace."

"Good. Have my carriage readied and a bag packed. After lunch, I'll be leaving to spend a few days at Wentworth Manor in Lincolnshire."

The color drained from the butler's ruddy face. "Alone, Your Grace?"

Warrick understood immediately. "I suppose I'll have to take the lads with me."

Wilson brightened. "I'll inform your valet, Your Grace."

Warrick got to his feet and made his way to the dining room. No doubt the food fight had already begun. He hoped Philip and Jenny Fortescue would still consider him a friend after spending a few days with his hellions as their guests.

GLACIAL EXPRESSION

The Beaufort town coach was roomy and well-sprung, the squabs plush. However, traveling with five rambunctious lads was like being trapped in a tombola drum. Threats of tossing them out at the next crossroads did nothing to stop the argument about who should sit closest to the windows. After only half an hour, every cravat was askew, including Warrick's. Tom had a fat lip courtesy of Charlie's fist. Tom had committed the unforgivable crime of throwing Charlie's cap out of the carriage when the latter shoved him away from the window.

Nothing for it but to call a halt and backtrack to retrieve the headgear.

Sweating, Warrick was tempted to climb into the rumble seat with Carlos as the journey resumed. Unfortunately, the Spaniard would then spend at least ten minutes swearing at his master in his own language. Carlos likely didn't realize Warrick knew he was swearing. A man couldn't live his whole life in Hull's dockland without learning how to curse in several languages. Warrick could well imagine the diatribe that would spew forth when they reached Raventhorpe and his valet set eyes on the disheveled lads.

Todos mis malditos esfuerzos para nada!
All my bloody hard work for nothing.

Warrick shrugged as the arguing continued. It seemed every effort to improve the behavior of his charges was going nowhere.

Entering the avenue leading to Wentworth Manor, he glanced over at the stables. Grooms were unhitching a handsome team of blacks from another carriage that bore Harrowby's crest. The Harcourts had come to visit. Perhaps he should have sent word of his coming rather than arriving unannounced. When his carriage came to a halt, he opened his mouth to warn the lads to be on their best behavior. Heedless, they tumbled out and rushed to the front door.

He hurried to catch up in time to see the butler surveying the scene before him as if eyeing a barrel of wriggling maggots. "Hop it," he commanded, his face reddening when he saw Warrick. "Take these mongrels round back, sir."

Clearly, Beckley did not remember him.

"My apologies, Beckley," he said. "Beaufort to see His Grace."

"Of course...er...Your Grace," the butler stammered as recognition dawned.

The gang didn't wait for permission to enter.

"Cor," Eddie exclaimed. "Look at yon statue's tits."

Loud guffaws ensued as the boys clustered around a

time-worn Greek goddess whose faded green fig leaf covered only her lower private parts.

"My wards," Warrick explained to the bewildered butler, praying none of the lads had the temerity to touch the statue's breasts.

The commotion brought Philip Fortescue striding into the foyer. "Warrick," he exclaimed, extending his hand. "What a pleasant surprise. Welcome."

Philip's friendship was obviously genuine. The presence of five unruly boys couldn't be considered *a pleasant surprise*, yet Philip seemed glad and slightly amused to see his unexpected visitors ogling marble breasts.

"I was just showing off my new laboratory," Philip said. "Why don't I give you the tour?"

Warrick had once visited Philip's laboratory in Hull's Infirmary and found it fascinating. "You're carrying on your research?" he asked, nervous about unleashing the orphans in a room filled with breakable objects.

"Yes. My wife's suggestion. Jenny will greet you later. She's upstairs with her mother."

"I noticed the carriage," Warrick replied. "I take it Lady Penelope came with the Harcourts."

"Actually, only Amelia accompanied her mother. She's in the laboratory awaiting my return."

A wave of heat rolled over Warrick. A pulse throbbed in his ears. "Wonderful," he exclaimed from a throat that was suddenly as dry as the desert.

AMELIA STARTLED when a group of exuberant boys burst into the laboratory, pushing and shoving each other. She didn't know them, but they reminded her of the Knowsley brothers. The flat caps seemed at odds with the quality of the rest of their clothing.

This was obviously not an acceptable way to enter a room full of important, fragile equipment. She stiffened her spine and assumed the facial expression that had stood her in good stead in Lancashire. The posture conveyed a strong message without the necessity of uttering a word.

She cleared her throat to get their attention.

It was as if lightning had struck. The racket ceased. Caps in hand, the boys clustered together with bare heads bowed.

Elation soared. She hadn't lost her touch. About to congratulate them for remembering their manners, the words died in her throat when Warrick Farrell entered with her brother-in-law.

She recalled that his father had recently passed and he was now a duke. "Your Grace," she mumbled, fervently hoping her trembling knees would support her when she rose from her curtsey. "My condolences."

He was everything she remembered. Tall, broad-shouldered, a powerful raven-haired presence.

"Warrick, please," he replied, taking her hand to help her rise. "Thank you for your condolences, Amelia. It's a delightful surprise to see you again."

The brogue and the callouses were gone, the nails manicured, but the warmth of his hand and the genuine pleasure in his green eyes sent desire spiraling up the back of her thighs and into her womb. The laboratory suddenly felt like an inferno. His effect on her senses hadn't diminished.

Sniggers from their audience served to jolt her back to reality. These lads must be the orphans Warrick had taken to Beaufort, and she was staring at him as if he were a god come down from Olympus. She quickly resumed her governess mask and the murmuring ceased.

∽

Warrick rarely found himself at a loss for words. Survival in the slums depended on a man keeping his wits about him. The revelation that he'd been made his father's heir was the last time he'd been gobsmacked.

Encountering Amelia Saxton so unexpectedly had been a shock, though his cock deemed it a very pleasant surprise. She was everything he remembered—tall, innocently alluring and round in all the right places.

Obviously not expecting to be in company, she wasn't wearing gloves. Her elusive perfume stole up his nostrils when he brushed a kiss on her warm knuckles. He considered the courtesy as ridiculously aristocratic and frivolous. Now, he was seized by an urge to lavish kisses the length of her arm.

Adding to his speechlessness was her apparent ease in taming the hellions without saying a word. He hoped she never turned that glacial expression on him.

"Won't you introduce me to these young gentlemen?" she said.

Gentlemen?

"Of course," he replied after another moment of confusion. "Boys, make your bow to Miss Saxton."

As each in turn mumbled his name and bowed politely, Warrick realized they had, in fact, paid attention to at least some of their tutors' lessons in proper behavior.

"Now, offer your respects to His Grace, the Duke of Wentworth," Amelia instructed in a voice that brooked no opposition. "This is his laboratory and I'm sure he would be happy to explain some of the experiments to you."

"Your Grace," they chimed in unison as they turned to Philip, eyes bright with expectation.

ROUGH EDGES

Philip's pride and confidence in his research shone through as he led the visitors through the laboratory. Amelia understood completely why her sister loved him. He was handsome, fit and intelligent. He had a sense of humor that wasn't in the least condescending. The perfect husband. Titled and wealthy.

She was very fond of Philip, but he held no appeal for her as a man. It was Warrick Farrell who made her heart flutter and caused quivering sensations in secret places. The insightful questions he asked about Philip's experiments showed a lively mind. Her brother-in-law was tall, but Warrick topped him by inches. He was titled and no doubt wealthy.

However, there was an earthiness to Warrick that Philip lacked. He'd learned to speak and dress like an aristocrat, but she'd wager he hadn't changed much on the inside. People could never leave their formative years completely behind. Eliza and Jenny were duchesses now, but they hadn't let the title nor the wealth go to their heads. They were still approachable, lovable, down-to-earth sisters—daughters of a genteel, impoverished family. She was confident the Saxton girls would always have that in common.

The orphan boys listened intently to scientific explanations beyond her understanding. She recognized that memories of what they'd experienced in the slums would shape them, no matter anyone's efforts to change that.

It would be the same for Warrick and it was disturbingly startling for Amelia to realize that his appeal lay in his rough edges.

∼

NOT FOR THE FIRST TIME, Philip's laboratory opened Warrick's eyes to the importance of a good education. He'd survived the slums on his wits, but there was so much more to life than just surviving. Philip was using his education to improve the lives of others. Warrick's only contribution to his fellow human beings was that he was trying to offer a bunch of miscreants a chance at a better life. Even in that endeavor, he was completely at sea, whereas Amelia had known instinctively how to handle his lads.

What was it about her that brought out the best in people? He felt real in her presence, not the imposter masquerading as a duke.

He was confident she would work wonders with his charges if she came to Cavendish Manor and took things in hand.

His body misunderstood. "Down, boy," he growled as an image of cavorting naked with Amelia surged into his thoughts—and his loins.

Therein lay the difficulty. He'd resolved to follow his father's advice and marry well. Amelia Saxton might be sister to two duchesses but she was a commoner nonetheless. He wanted her, and it would be difficult not to act on his attraction if she lived in his home. However, marriage to a commoner, a governess in his employ, would sully the reputation of the dukedom he'd never wanted. The nobility would be even more convinced that Beaufort had been out of his mind when he named Warrick his heir.

Many aristocrats kept mistresses, but he doubted Amelia would agree to that. He might be a child of the slums but he knew what honor was. If and when he married, he intended to be faithful to his wife. He had only to remember his own mother's fate as an abandoned mistress to be certain he'd never consign Amelia to that life.

∼

"They seem interested in science," Amelia remarked, though she got the feeling Warrick's mind was wandering elsewhere.

Not that she had been able to concentrate on

anything but his presence. She supposed she should feel intimidated by his size. He towered over her, but there was a gentleness about him that made her feel safe and protected.

He could squash her like a bug if he'd a mind to, but she knew he would never raise his hand to a woman. Most people likely thought a man who'd grown up in the slums could have no notion of honor, but that wasn't true of Warrick Farrell. The mere fact he was trying to share his good fortune with a crew of orphans proved his worth.

She loved and respected her ducal brothers-in-law. They were both engaged in endeavors aimed at improving the lives of the less fortunate in society. However, she suspected neither Alex Harcourt nor Philip Fortescue would willingly take on five unruly urchins.

"Yes," Warrick replied. "I should bear that in mind when we return to Cavendish Manor. Nothing holds their attention for long."

A host of suggestions came to mind, but Warrick might think her too presumptuous. Jenny's arrival with Lady Penelope in tow saved her.

"Beaufort," her sister exclaimed, eyeing the boys. "This is a surprise."

"Arrived unannounced," their mother huffed, waving a hand at the lads. "And who are these creatures?"

"We're glad to see Warrick and his wards any time they wish to visit," Philip replied.

Warrick bowed to Philip's duchess. "Your Grace," he said, hoping the lads were paying attention.

"We're all equals here," she replied. "Please call me Jenny."

"Then I insist you use my given name. I can't seem to get used to being referred to as Beaufort."

"We were saddened to hear of your father's untimely death," she said, laying a sympathetic hand on his arm.

"Thank you," he replied. Her genuine regret touched him but he wished it was Amelia's hand resting on his arm.

He startled when Mrs. Saxton shoved her ring-bedecked hand under his nose. "Lady Penelope," she said. "Her Grace's mother."

Ignoring the deliberate rudeness, Warrick brushed a kiss on her knuckles. "My lady," he said. "We have met before."

"I do recall," she replied haughtily. "You were kneeling in the dirt. I see you were serious about attempting to educate these ragamuffins."

"He was kneeling on the ground because he was trying to save my father's life, Madam," Philip protested.

Fingers crossed behind his back, Warrick turned to his lads, praying they would prove his faith in them was justified. "Gentlemen, make yourselves known to the duchess and Lady Penelope."

He breathed again when, one by one, they did a creditable job of bowing and properly addressing Jenny Fortescue.

There was a subtle contempt in their voices when

they introduced themselves to Lady Penelope, but she was so intent on making sure not one of them touched her hand, he doubted she was aware they'd taken the measure of her disdain.

DIVIDE AND CONQUER

Mealtimes with the orphans at Cavendish Manor were not for the faint of heart. They'd toned down their bad manners when Warrick's father was still alive. He'd indulged them to a degree, reminding Warrick that one couldn't expect miracles overnight.

They apparently assumed his death meant *carte blanche* had been declared on belching, slurping and talking with one's mouth full. Warrick finally lost his temper completely when the farting began. In pointing out such behavior was not permitted at table, he made the mistake of referring to it as *breaking wind*. This resulted in hysterical laughter and more offensive odors. He compounded his error by using the term *flatulence*. It immediately became a competition to see who could produce the loudest and foulest *flat lances*.

As he ushered his miscreants into the dining room of Wentworth Manor, he could only pray the presence of other adults would have a sobering effect. He and Carlos had a battle royal on their hands when they'd insisted the caps were not permitted during an evening meal in the house of another duke.

The duchess, Lady Penelope and Amelia were already seated—with an empty chair between each of them. "Amelia's suggestion for the seating plan," Philip whispered close to Warrick's ear. "Divide and conquer."

Then, he took charge. "Kenny, you're between Her Grace and Lady Penelope."

Eyes downcast and shoulders hunched, Kenny slid into his place and shrank into the chair.

"Charlie, you're on Lady Penelope's other side. Tim, you're between my wife and Miss Saxton."

Relief brightened Tim's face. Charlie cringed like a felon sentenced to the gallows.

"Tom will sit between Miss Saxton and my fellow duke, and Eddie, place of honor between the Duke of Beaufort and myself."

Eddie's chest swelled. The rest glared at him.

"Let's say grace together, shall we?" Philip suggested. "Bless us, O, Lord," he began.

To Warrick's utter amazement, the lads joined in with everyone else. "And these Thy gifts which we are about to receive from Thy bounty. Through Christ Our Lord, Amen."

As the meal progressed without so much as a peep from any of the lads, Warrick smiled gratefully at Amelia. She'd known how to avert a potential disaster. Perhaps it was the presence of females that had done the trick. He and the male tutors he'd employed had failed. He could spend years looking for an equally capable governess.

The boys needed Amelia at Cavendish Manor. And so did he. No titled lady would consider marrying a man with a houseful of delinquents.

∽

Amelia stood before the cheval mirror in the third floor guest bedroom where she and Jenny had once shared a bed on the occasion of their first visit to Wentworth. Still feeling the glow from Warrick's smile of approval at dinner, she didn't feel the least bit tired.

"I look like an old maid in this nightgown," she declared, startling when Jenny entered the bedchamber.

"You're too beautiful to ever be an old maid," her sister scolded.

"It's like a shroud," Amelia insisted.

"We can go shopping for something a little more feminine in Raventhorpe on the morrow, if you wish."

Amelia shrugged, the glow fast disappearing. "What's the point? I'm fated to be a spinster who lives with her increasingly cantankerous mother."

"Rubbish. We finally have a few minutes to spend together. Don't be down in the dumps."

"Easy for you to say. You've already got a handsome husband who dotes on you."

Jenny chivvied her into bed. " You're just feeling sorry for yourself. I see the way Beaufort looks at you."

"But he's a duke now, not just Warrick Farrell."

"May I remind you I am married to a duke?"

"It's different. Warrick can't marry a commoner, even if he wanted me for his wife."

"I'm sure he does after the way you handled his charges."

"I think that's the only reason Warrick seemed pleased. I could never go to Beaufort just to take the boys in hand. It would be too difficult to see him married to another."

Jenny perched on the edge of the mattress. "Well, selfishly, I prefer you not run off to Derbyshire. I need your help here redecorating this enormous house."

Amelia's spirits revived. "It will be great fun. Shopping in Raventhorpe sounds like a good idea."

Jenny nodded. "We might even have to go further afield to find tasteful items. Scunthorpe or Lincoln, perhaps."

"I think the first thing to replace are those awful statues in the foyer."

Jenny laughed. "I agree. And the urns."

"And the tarnished mirrors."

Amelia sobered when a daunting thought struck. "I shouldn't say this, but I wish we could choose your new refurbishments without Mama. She actually likes the statues."

∽

AFTER A RESTLESS NIGHT plagued by indecision and the pillow-fighting going on in the adjoining chamber, Warrick warned his charges he wouldn't tolerate any shenanigans during breakfast.

He needn't have worried. One look from Amelia Saxton transformed them into perfectly behaved angels.

His dilemma only worsened. She was definitely the person to take charge of the lads' education. But he was drawn to her—more than drawn in fact. The urge to pull down the bodice of her gown and swipe his tongue along the swell of her lovely globes drained every drop of saliva from his mouth. The prospect of kissing tempting lips had his cock in full salute. Seeing her every day would be torture. Could he bear it for the sake of the orphans' futures?

Warrick and his host were scheduled to meet this morning in Philip's study. He anticipated a long and difficult session. It would be hard enough revealing his illiteracy to his fellow duke. One thing was for sure, Amelia must never discover his secret.

It was perhaps fortuitous then that the duchess and her sister planned to spend the day shopping in Raventhorpe. Out of sight, out of mind, he hoped.

BOGGED DOWN

"Well," Amelia sighed as she and Jenny stepped down from the Wentworth carriage with the aid of a footman. "Raventhorpe is quaint, but I doubt we'll find any shops. The beer house seems to be the only commercial establishment."

"Nowt much else 'erabouts, septin' farms, Yer Grace," James Footman informed them. "We mun go on to Scunthorpe if thee wants shops."

"Sorry, Amelia," Jenny said, gesturing to the rutted lane that apparently served as Raventhorpe's main thoroughfare. "I only came here once on the way to the manor."

"And I expect you were paying more attention to Philip than to the scenery."

"You know me well," her sister conceded with a coy smile.

Amelia scanned the bucolic scene. "Why don't we go

for a walk? The meadows beyond that stile seem to go on for miles."

"Good idea," Jenny replied. "James can help us over the stile then stay with the carriage until we return."

"Beggin' yer pardon, Yer Grace," James replied. "'Is Grace'll 'ave mi 'ead if I leave thee alone in a field."

"He's right," Amelia said. "We might need him if we encounter a ferocious bull."

The color drained from James' face.

"She's teasing you," Jenny explained. "But perhaps you should accompany us."

~

CLUTCHING THE CRUCIAL DOCUMENTS, Warrick accompanied Philip into his study and sat in the leather chair his host indicated. He wasn't looking forward to the humiliating experience of revealing his inability to read and write. His background had already mired his new dukedom in difficulties. "Your duchess and her sister have gone shopping in the village," he said in an effort to delay the inevitable.

"Yes, although I doubt they'll find anything they want to buy. It's basically a farming community."

"I recall a physician came from there when your father was shot."

"Yes. He's elderly and retired, but capable nonetheless."

"I recall," Warrick replied, realizing too late he had repeated himself.

"I never did thank you properly for your efforts to save him," Philip said.

"No need. I'm just sorry the ball eventually killed him."

"But your quick actions gave him extra months that I believe he truly enjoyed. My mother is very grateful for her memories of the time they spent together in Bath."

"Marvelous invention, the Bath chair."

"Indeed."

"Do you still have it?"

"Yes. Behind the screen over there. I felt it belonged in this study where he spent so much of his life."

Warrick nodded, his innards in knots.

"Enough small talk, my friend. Let's take a look at those papers before you crush them beyond recognition."

Relief mingled with humiliation. Warrick thought he'd successfully hidden his problem, but Philip evidently suspected. "I..."

"I made assumptions," his fellow duke admitted. "And I apologize for that. I should have realized you never had the opportunity for an education. I thought Beaufort..."

"I was too ashamed to tell him," Warrick confessed. "I thought I'd have time to learn to read and write by myself, never dreaming my father would die so soon."

"So, the documents are of immediate concern," Philip said. "Matters of inheritance, I suppose?"

"Yes, but I can't use my mark where my signature should be. I'd quickly become a laughing stock."

"I can guide your hand," Philip offered after giving the problem some thought.

"You can have no idea how grateful I would be," Warrick replied.

"However, that's a stop-gap measure. In the long run, you'll have to acquire the skills."

"I know. I may look and talk like a duke but, in reality, I'm just as ill-suited for this life as my lads."

"Nonsense. I believe you've the makings of an excellent duke. You bring a different perspective to the title. The British aristocracy needs a shock to its system. You're an intelligent fellow. What you lack is a good teacher."

Warrick didn't like the suggestive gleam in Philip's eyes. "If you're thinking of Miss Saxton, I could never reveal my ignorance to her."

"You underestimate Amelia if you believe she would think less of you."

"I've been thinking of inviting her to be the boys' governess."

"She's probably the ideal person," Philip agreed.

"I'll ask her," Warrick decided against his better judgment. "But I prefer she not know about my problem yet."

"As you wish. Now, first things first. Let's see to those documents."

～

The sisters and their escort hadn't walked far from the stile, but Amelia could see Jenny was tiring. The weak sun hadn't yet dried the morning dew. The slippery grass made for slow going. "We should turn back," she said.

"Aye, Yer Grace," James Footman agreed nervously as he trudged behind.

"Just a bit further," Jenny insisted. "To the farm over there, perhaps."

"Yonder Matthias Greg's farm," James said. "'E keeps pigs."

Jenny and Amelia held their noses when a pungent odor confirmed the footman's warning.

"I'd love to see piglets," Jenny said as they approached the outbuildings.

The trio halted abruptly when the ground underfoot turned boggy.

Amelia's heart stopped beating when an enormous, mud-encrusted pig emerged from a lean-to and trotted toward them, stubby legs moving its considerable bulk with surprising speed.

"Oh, my," Jenny exclaimed, clutching Amelia's arm. "He doesn't look friendly."

To his credit, James was obviously thinking more clearly than his ladies. "Be'ind me, Yer Grace," he hissed, grasping his mistress' arm.

Unfortunately, Jenny lost her balance as a result and slipped in the mud, dragging Amelia with her.

James tore off his white wig. Waving it and shouting at the top of his lungs, he ran toward the charging pig.

The grunting beast skidded to a halt, turned tail and retreated.

Wallowing in the mud, Amelia and Jenny giggled at the comical sight of a liveried servant instilling fear into the heart of an enraged pig by means of a wig.

They were laughing heartily when the angry farmer emerged from the farmhouse.

James turned to run back toward them, apparently more afraid of Matthias Greg than of the pig. He too slipped in the mud.

Amelia knew it was wrong to laugh at another's misfortune, but she and her sister couldn't seem to stop. It was as though they were once more the mischievous Saxton girls of years ago.

INDECIPHERABLE

W arrick and Philip had just exited the study when a commotion in the foyer drew their attention. Accompanied by a footman, the duchess and Amelia entered, their hair and faces daubed with mud. The women's gowns and the footman's livery were caked with it. Muddy footprints dotted the tiled flooring. Amelia and her sister were in high spirits, but Philip apparently failed to see the humor. He rushed to his duchess' side.

"I'm perfectly fine," she panted, her face beet red. "We encountered an angry pig."

"You allowed my wife to be injured?" he accused the footman.

"No," Amelia interjected, stepping forward to defend the servant. As she did so, her shoe slipped on the wet tiles. Panic flared in her eyes as she struggled to stay upright.

Warrick dropped the dossier containing his documents, reached out and caught her before she fell.

For what seemed an eternity, he stared into wide hazel eyes—until her heaving bosom snagged his attention.

Philip's loud cough jolted him back to reality, but had no effect on the throbbing at his groin.

"Thank you," Amelia breathed, her face red as he set her on her feet. "Oh, your papers. The mud."

Before he had time to react, she'd slipped from his grasp and was on her knees gathering up his scattered documents.

He knelt beside her, but she'd already seen the nature of the dossier's contents. He prayed she'd noticed nothing untoward about the scrawled signature that looked like a fly with ink on its legs had crawled across the parchment. He had difficulty accepting that the meandering black line represented his name but Philip assured him most noblemen's signatures were indecipherable.

Unable to meet Amelia's curious gaze, he gently retrieved the papers from her hands, picked up the remainder and stuffed the lot into the dossier.

"We seem to be fated to be on our knees together," he said as he and the footman helped her rise.

"The carriage will likely need cleaning," Jenny announced as she lifted her skirts and flounced toward the staircase.

Directed at her husband, Jenny's cheeky remark snapped Amelia out of her trance.

PHILIP CONTINUED to glare angrily at the footman. Following her sister's lead, Amelia mounted the stairs to her chamber. They were still giddy over their misadventure, but the episode with Warrick's documents tempered Amelia's glee.

They were obviously important papers to do with his inheritance of the dukedom. Perhaps that explained Warrick's consternation when he realized she'd seen them. Women had no right to even be aware of such matters. But, why had he brought them to Philip? And what was bothersome about the signature scrawled next to the seal?

More distracting was the overwhelming excitement that surged when Warrick caught her before she fell. She might have drowned in the mesmerizing emerald depths of his gaze. An ache of wanting blossomed inside her.

She only half listened to the little French maid supervising the preparation of her bath, embarrassed that her nipples seemed harder and darker than usual when the girl helped her undress.

Soaking in the tub, she closed her eyes and pondered the enigma of Warrick Farrell. She suspected he might offer her the position of governess to his boys. It was tempting to accept. She was confident she could prepare the orphans for worthwhile careers. However, it would be impossible to hide her feelings for her employer. Memories of her narrow escape from Lancashire made her shudder, although Warrick was nothing like the predatory Knowsley. Still, it would be difficult to resist her attraction to him.

As the water cooled, her mind wandered to the odd-looking signature on the documents. Why bring them to Wentworth? Panic darkened Warrick's eyes when...

She sat bolt upright when the truth dawned. "He's illiterate," she exclaimed.

"*Comment, milady?*" the maid asked.

"*Rien,*" Amelia replied, wondering how she could have been so obtuse. The realization changed everything. She cared for Warrick too much to allow him to struggle alone with his burden. If he asked, she would go to Beaufort—to help the boys, yes, but he would never be accepted by his peers if he couldn't read or write. It was up to her. She'd simply have to put her personal feelings aside and prepare him to take his rightful place in society.

~

Aware he was in danger of being late for dinner, Warrick dithered as Carlos fiddled with his cravat. What kind of duke couldn't make up his mind about a simple matter?

"*Problema, Vuestra Merced?*" his valet asked, evidently sensing his turmoil.

"I want to make the best decision for the boys," he replied. "They need a governess."

"*Sí,*" Carlos replied. "*La señorita* Saxton."

Warrick shook his head. Even his valet had seen Amelia's suitability for the job. "She's more than qualified," he agreed.

"And she good for you, *también,*" Carlos added. "*Perfecta!*"

Warrick wasn't sure if the Spaniard was referring to

Miss Saxton or to the cravat, but his valet bustled him out the door before he could delve deeper. It was for the best. He'd always depended on his own good judgment, and surely dukes didn't seek the opinion of their valets?

Tempted to ease the tight cravat away from his throat before it strangled him, he popped his head into the boys' chamber. "Your meals are on the way. I'm trusting you to behave."

"Why can't we nosh int' dining room?" Eddie asked.

"Because the adults need a break from your shenanigans."

Muffled grumbling greeted this truth.

Hoping he'd said enough, Warrick hurried down the stairs and entered the drawing room. Everyone had already gathered for a glass of sherry before dinner.

"Here's Beaufort, at last," Philip exclaimed with a smile as he directed a footman to serve him.

Warrick took the glass from the footman's tray, anxious not to pay too much attention to Amelia and her sister who were sitting side by side on the settee. Looking at Amelia Saxton tended to muddle his thoughts. Both women were now mud-free. That led his unruly imagination to picture Amelia in a tub of hot water...the soap bubbles hiding her...

Get a grip, man.

The cravat suddenly felt tighter. Was he coming down with something? He'd lived so long in the filth of dockland, perhaps his body couldn't cope with cleanliness.

One look at Philip's raised eyebrow put paid to that ridiculous notion.

He'd participated in many risky ventures—most of them illegal. Getting caught would have led to gaol, or transportation, or worse. Yet, he'd never before felt like he teetered on the edge of a precipice.

Amelia Saxton had him tied in knots.

"Can I impose upon you to escort the Saxton ladies into dinner?" Philip asked as he offered his own arm to his duchess.

"Of course," Warrick replied, relieved to return the full glass of sherry to the tray. Liquor had destroyed his mother's life and left him with a determination not to indulge in intoxicating beverages. Six months as a nobleman had taught him that spirits would be difficult to avoid. Aristocrats loved their brandy.

Amelia smiled as she took his arm.

Lady Penelope did not.

They had barely entered the dining room when Beckley appeared. "Forgive the intrusion, Your Graces. There's a problem with the young men."

Warrick gritted his teeth. Trays had been brought to the orphans' chamber so the adults might dine in peace. He might have expected an argument of some sort. "I'll go," he said.

"I'll come with you," Amelia replied.

WILL SHE, WON'T SHE?

Reluctant to remove her hand from the solid strength of Warrick's arm after they'd mounted the stairs, Amelia nevertheless called a halt outside the boys' chamber. Raised voices and sneering laughter were sure signs an argument was in progress. "Let me go in first," she said breathlessly, hoping he thought it was the exercise that had robbed her of the ability to breathe properly.

"Are you sure?" he asked, though she detected a hint of relief in the question.

She suspected self-confidence had helped Warrick Farrell survive his former life. Yet, he was clearly uncertain about how to handle his orphans in a world alien to the one they'd all known. He wanted only the best for his urchins. She could help him in his noble endeavor.

Nodding, she turned the doorknob, entered the chamber and slowly closed the door behind her. She waited for the squabbling quintet to notice her.

It took a moment or two for the shouting to die down and another moment for utter silence to fall.

It was the first time she'd seen them capless. Mouths agape, they looked very young and vulnerable. She suddenly understood why they insisted on wearing the headgear. The flat caps were their protective armor.

"I'll get one of the servants to collect your trays if you're finished," she said calmly.

Probably expecting to be chastised, they continued to gape.

Kenny spoke first. "Er...no, Miss Saxton. We ain't done."

"Then can you make a little less noise? The servants have enough to do without being bothered, and I would like to eat my meal in peace."

"Aye, Miss Saxton," they mumbled in unison.

"Gentleman normally say *Yes*, not *Aye*," she said, sounding too much like her mother. "Take your places at the table , if you please."

"Yes, Miss Saxton," they replied as they hurried to obey. "Sorry, Miss Saxton."

It occurred to her these lads had known very little affection in their short lives. "If you wish, I'll come back later to make sure you're tucked in."

The longing in bright young eyes nigh on broke her heart. "Until later," she said as she left them.

"It's too quiet," Warrick whispered as she closed the door softly.

"They're eating," she replied.

"This I have to see," he replied, reaching for the doorknob.

Without thinking, she pressed her hand to his chest. "Leave it. I promised to come up later to tuck them in."

She couldn't seem to remove her hand, though touching a peer of the realm without permission was a huge social *faux pas*.

Her nipples tingled when he covered her hand with his. His heart was beating even faster than her own. It proved impossible to drag her gaze from his warm, green eyes. He leaned closer. She was certain he meant to kiss her. She shouldn't allow it, should she?

Instead, he murmured, "The boys need you at Cavendish Manor, Amelia. Will you be their governess?"

It was what she wanted, what she'd hoped for. The longing in his eyes, the warmth of his hand and her suspicion about his illiteracy—all spoke of his need. However, he'd only mentioned the lads. He might not welcome her interference in his personal life. Her fluttering heart and the aching desire for his kiss were clear signs of the danger she was in. Furthermore, she'd promised to assist Jenny with the refurbishment of Wentworth Manor. "I'll consider it," she replied, withdrawing her hand.

She wanted to snatch back the haughty reply when the light in his eyes dimmed.

"May I escort you back downstairs, Miss Saxton?" he asked.

It was too late to remind him that he'd always called her Amelia. She was the one who'd erected the barrier. Perhaps that was a good thing. "Of course, Your Grace," she replied.

Amelia's haughty reply kicked Warrick squarely in the gut. Obviously, he'd gone about things in entirely the wrong way. How else to explain her sudden change of demeanor? He'd slipped from *Warrick* to *Your Grace*. He'd almost kissed those tempting full lips—another close call. Being a duke was fraught with pitfalls. Life in the slums had been much simpler. If he wanted to kiss a lass, he did. Now, there were all kinds of missteps to navigate. At least she hadn't been aware of his throbbing arousal. The cool and collected man who'd always kept control of his male urges became a raging bull in the presence of Amelia Saxton.

Amelia was a commoner. So was he, although the circumstances of her birth and upbringing placed her far above the reach of Warrick Farrell, slum dweller—but unsuitable for His Grace, the Duke of Beaufort. The irony of it.

He'd truly believed she would gladly accept the position at Cavendish Manor. He'd even toyed with the notion of confessing his illiteracy and asking for her help. Thank goodness he'd kept his mouth shut. She apparently wasn't as attracted to him as he thought. That was a good thing if he was destined to marry a titled heiress. Wasn't it?

If he were still plain old Warrick Farrell, he'd take hold of the delicate hand whose warmth penetrated the sleeve of his frock-coat and speak openly of his dilemma. But aristocrats frowned on that kind of thing.

THE FOOD SERVED during dinner was probably wonderful. Everyone else thought so. Amelia had no idea what she was eating. She couldn't bring herself to look at Warrick across the table. He barely said a word, except to let his hosts know he and the boys would be leaving at first light the next morning.

"Surely you can stay a day or two longer," Philip said.

"Unfortunately," he replied. "My presence is required at home, and we don't wish to impose any longer."

"I should think not," Lady Penelope interjected.

"Just as Amelia was making progress with your lads," Jenny exclaimed, glaring at her mother. "You should consider employing her as their governess."

Trust the plain-speaking Jenny to set the fox among the hens. Had Amelia been seated next to her sister, she would have kicked her under the table. As it was, heat flooded her from head to toe.

"I did offer her the position," Warrick replied, avoiding her gaze. "She seems reluctant."

Gooseflesh marched across Amelia's nape when curious eyes shifted to her. Didn't Warrick realize he was putting her on the spot?

"Why would you refuse such an offer?" Jenny asked.

Apparently sensing the tension, Philip cleared his throat, but his wife wasn't to be silenced. "You're exactly what those boys need."

"I agree," Warrick said. "But I fully understand her prior commitment to helping you with the renovations here."

"Nonsense," Jenny retorted. "I have staff to help with that. It would be fun to do it with you, Amelia, but this is the kind of position you've always wanted."

Amelia squirmed. As the youngest, she'd taken a back seat and been content to let her older sisters be the center of attention. Resenting that Warrick had perhaps unwittingly forced her into making a decision, she plucked up her courage and looked across at him. The plea in his eyes swept away her intention to refuse. He was thinking only of the boys whereas she was being selfish. "If you truly don't need me at Wentworth," she said. "I am willing to go to Derbyshire."

IVANHOE

Warrick borrowed a handsome gelding so he could ride back to Cavendish Manor. He recognized his cowardice in leaving Amelia alone in the carriage with the lads. He still wasn't sure how she truly felt about taking on the job of governess to the gang. He'd never survive hours in a cramped carriage without succumbing to the urge to touch her.

To his surprise, Eddie asked to ride pillion and Kenny insisted he'd rather sit beside the driver. This left some room for Carlos to make the journey inside instead of clinging to the boot.

After three hours, the driver shouted his intention to pull off the road into the courtyard of an inn in the village of Retford. Warrick nodded his agreement. The horses needed the respite. He'd been pleased when Eddie expressed a desire to ride with him. Maddeningly, he'd spent three hours wishing it was Amelia clinging to his back. She wouldn't have whined constantly about her bum being rubbed raw. When the lad slipped off the horse, Warrick was tempted to suggest he sit in the water trough for an hour. Instead, he told him to try harder to listen during the daily riding lessons.

Kenny climbed down from the driver's seat and crowed about what a marvelous time he'd had. He taunted Eddie about his sore posterior. Fisticuffs seemed imminent.

At that moment, the carriage door opened. Carlos emerged, let down the steps and assisted Amelia Saxton to alight. He recalled how embarrassingly disheveled and frazzled he'd been after the journey to Wentworth. Amelia looked as fresh and perfectly groomed as she had when they'd set off—not a hair out of place, the ribbons of her bonnet still tied in a jaunty bow beneath her chin.

Charlie emerged from the coach and proffered an arm. "Allow me to accompany you, Miss Saxton," he said.

Carlos must have noticed Warrick's look of amazement. "*Libro*," he said, as if that explained everything.

"A book?" Warrick asked.

"*Sì*. She read *Ivanhoe*. They were like...er...*esclavos*."

Warrick had heard of the popular novel written by Walter Scott. He suddenly wished he'd ridden in the carriage so he too could have been enthralled by Amelia's voice reading tales of medieval knights.

"It was a choice between that and *The Monster*," Amelia said, smoothing non-existent creases in her skirts as she joined them.

She might consider him a monster if she could read his lecherous thoughts about the long legs beneath those skirts.

"Philip told me he met the author," she added. "He offered to lend me his copy. But I decided on *Ivanhoe* since I haven't yet read *The Monster*. No use giving the boys nightmares."

To Warrick's further humbled amazement, Eddie and Kenny had left off bickering and were nodding their agreement with Amelia's wise words.

They spent over an hour in Retford exploring the busy market where they enjoyed pork pies and mash. They were persuaded to sample a glass of sarsaparilla, a new beverage touted by the temperance movement. Warrick sympathized with the boys' grimaces and gagging noises and was willing to overlook their only departure from gentlemanly behavior. He could almost believe they were a family—a happy couple and their sons wandering from one market stall to another. The notion filled him with contentment.

Still, he was uneasy; an argument would surely break out when they resumed their journey.

∼

"I suspect Eddie has had enough horse riding for today," Amelia said as everyone gathered to resume the journey. "Would anyone else like to ride with His Grace?"

Kenny shook his head. "I want a turn at listening to the tales of Sir Heave-Ho."

"Ivanhoe," Charlie amended. "And I want to listen too."

"Me an' all," Tim and Tom chimed together.

"Me too," she reminded them.

"Yes, Miss Saxton," they replied.

Amelia was pleased Charlie had corrected Kenny without belittling him, and she was delighted they all wanted to listen to more of Walter Scott's adventure story. "Perhaps Carlos wouldn't mind riding with the duke," she suggested, alarmed when the color drained from the Spaniard's leathery complexion.

"*Cab...all...o?*" he stammered, backing away from the gelding. "No, no, *señorita*. I sit with driver."

Amelia supposed she shouldn't blame him. Never having learned to ride, she wasn't comfortable around horses either. Although, it might be exciting to ride behind Warrick, her arms entwined round his waist...

She dismissed the ludicrous notion as heat swept over her. "Foolish girl," she muttered under her breath.

"Can you manage with all of them?" Warrick asked.

"Of course," she replied. "There'll be some wonderful views once we get closer to the Peak District. I'm sure they'll enjoy the scenery."

∽

AMELIA MAY HAVE HELD THE LADS' attention with *Ivanhoe*, but Warrick seriously doubted they'd be interested in scenic views. He'd been so busy keeping the peace on the way to Wentworth, he'd barely had a chance to spare a glance at the countryside through which they traveled.

She'd called it the Peak District. He really ought to learn more about Derbyshire. He was probably the only duke in the county. Riding around the estate was all very well, but he'd have to venture further afield, *broaden his horizons* as his father was wont to say.

He felt blessed to have fond memories of the man who'd sired him. He was glad to be free of the resentment he'd borne all his life. It had shaped his view of the world. Now, he knew that not all aristocrats were selfish snobs. The change in his circumstances had brought challenges, but his father believed he was equal to them. As he mounted the gelding, Warrick resolved to do his best to live up to that belief. He was more confident of success now he had Amelia to help him.

WELCOME TO CAVENDISH

Amelia was able to enjoy distant views of the Peak District without interruptions. The effort of acting like polite young men had worn out her charges. They'd fallen asleep by the time the carriage passed through Belper. She too was tired, but recognized that apprehension had as much to do with her exhaustion as the journey. Warrick had embarked on a new life. She wanted to help him and his orphans succeed in that life, but it would be too easy to become more attached to him than she already was. When he eventually found his heiress, she'd have to seek another position. Hopefully, by then, her efforts to prepare the boys for a successful future would have borne fruit.

The landscape reminded her a little of the Yorkshire Dales. She'd always found hiking in the fresh air a good way to clear one's head. If things got too stressful at Cavendish Manor, she'd simply go for a long walk. "Come to think on it," she whispered. "The lads would benefit from exploring the hills and dales of Derbyshire."

Satisfied with the idea, she clenched her jaw and fisted her hands as they passed through wrought iron gates. Her spirits lifted when a charming house came into view.

Cavendish Manor didn't possess the stately grandeur of Harrowby Hall, nor was it as large as Wentworth. Amelia guessed the two-story dwelling was built of gray stone, though some sort of creeping vine covered the entire façade in lush greenery. She counted fourteen mullioned windows in all and there seemed to be only two chimneys.

The carriage came to a halt in a large front courtyard dotted with topiary bushes. Eager to alight, she paused to watch Warrick dismount. Her mouth went dry. She knew he must have learned to ride since coming to Derbyshire, but he dismounted with athletic grace. Long legs...

"We're 'ome!" Eddie shouted, bringing her crashing back to earth.

~

WARRICK HAD BEEN IMPRESSED with Cavendish Manor from the moment he first saw his new home. While certainly grander than any place he'd ever lived, the house built in the Georgian era wasn't ostentatious. It looked more like a posh dwelling rather than a ducal manor. Once he got to know his father a little better, he recognized that the house reflected James Hastings' simpler tastes perfectly.

There were servants, of course, but not so many that Warrick hadn't soon learned their names. At first, they'd eyed him cautiously, but quickly made him feel at home when they realized the duke was proud of him. Warrick was pleased to hear Eddie's declaration that indicated he looked upon Cavendish as his home. It occurred to Warrick that he too felt a sense of belonging he'd never felt for any place he'd lived.

As he dismounted, he hoped Amelia would be happy within the walls of the first home he'd ever been proud of.

The lads were pushing and shoving each other but at least they were vying for the right to assist their new governess as she stepped down from the carriage.

Jealousy tightened his throat. He recognized it was foolish but reasoned it was *his* right to welcome her. Apparently sensing his intent, the boys fell back.

"Welcome to Cavendish Manor, Miss Saxton," he said, aware the lads were still within earshot.

Amelia took his hand. "It's a lovely house," she replied.

The touch of her delicate hand was enough to send heat soaring up his spine. Her smile turned the heat to molten desire.

Unable to let go, he stared at her lips and realized too late he should never have brought her here.

Carlos' sudden appearance beside them broke the spell. "I introduce you, *Señorita* Saxton," he said, bowing at the waist.

"I'd be grateful," she said, withdrawing her hand to place it on the valet's arm. "Excuse us, Your Grace."

"Bloody Spaniard," Warrick growled as he watched them disappear into the house.

AMELIA'S INTRODUCTION to the hastily assembled staff of Cavendish Manor was one of the oddest experiences she'd ever had. It quickly became apparent Carlos didn't know the names of the other servants. Looking down his long nose at the valet, a tall man whose attire proclaimed him to be the butler, took over. "Mr. Wilson," he droned. "And you are?"

"This is our new governess," Eddie explained politely. "Miss Saxton."

Gaping at the boy, Wilson raised an eyebrow as relief slackened his stern features. "I see. Welcome to Cavendish, Miss Saxton."

Amelia could well imagine the merry dance the lads had led this very proper butler. "Thank you, Mr. Wilson," she replied.

"Just Wilson will suffice," he said with what might have been an attempt at a smile.

Amelia was hopeful she had made a friend.

"I'll take over from here, Wilson," Warrick said as he joined them.

Amelia prayed there might come a day when his deep voice didn't cause peculiar sensations to run rampant in secret places. She tried resolutely to will away the heat rising in her face. She'd never been prone to blushing, but now...Perhaps the long journey had simply been too much.

"I'll begin by introducing my housekeeper, Mrs. Knight," Warrick said.

"Miss Saxton," the diminutive woman replied

politely enough, though she made no attempt to curtsey. Obviously, a governess was ranked as a fellow servant. It reminded Amelia of her first day in the Knowsley household.

"I suggest Master Block's former chamber for the moment," Warrick instructed.

"I concur, Your Grace," Mrs. Knight replied before chivvying two maids to accompany her as she headed for the staircase in the center of the foyer.

Warrick introduced the remaining footmen, maids and kitchen staff by name. Amelia was impressed but not surprised. Warrick had none of the snobbish disdain for servants that many aristocrats exhibited.

"Miss Saxton will join the boys and myself for dinner," he informed Wilson.

The butler and the cook frowned. It seemed they too thought of her as a servant. "Very well, Your Grace," Wilson replied.

Amelia knew something the staff didn't. Warrick could have only one reason for wanting her at the dinner table—to ensure the lads behaved. The realization was both amusing and disappointing.

INQUIRING MIND

"Goodnight, gentlemen," Warrick said in response to his orphans' request for permission to leave the table.

He was tempted to smile at the gobsmacked expressions on the faces of the footmen who had come to expect the gang's unruly behavior.

"Goodnight," Amelia echoed. "I'll be up to see you shortly."

There was some jostling when they reached the doorway, but it was nothing compared to what had transpired before.

"I didn't want to offer to tuck them in again," Amelia whispered. "That might have embarrassed them in front of the servants."

"They understood," Warrick replied. "To be honest, even when we all lived together in Hull, it never occurred to me they might crave such a simple thing."

"They are just little boys at heart," she replied.

A heavy silence ensued. Warrick wished he'd never mentioned goodnight kisses. It wasn't only little boys who craved Amelia's kisses.

"Is your room satisfactory?" he asked though he itched to tell her how thankful he was she'd agreed to come to Cavendish.

"It's charming," she replied. "It will look a little less bare once I unpack a few of my things."

He took that as a good omen. She evidently saw the governess position as a long-term engagement.

Henry Footman held her chair as she rose. "Do you think it's too soon for me to say goodnight to them?" she asked. "I wouldn't want to intrude if they are still...er..."

Warrick liked seeing the proper Miss Saxton a little off kilter. It hinted at a freer spirit beneath the prim exterior. As he got to his feet, he wondered if the blush spread to her breasts, but the gown's high neck thwarted his thirst to know. "I'm sure Carlos has them in nightshirts already," he assured her. "He's the one person they seem to fear, probably because he swears at them in Spanish when they misbehave. They don't know what to make of him."

He cursed himself as she averted her eyes and the blush deepened. Gentlemen didn't speak of nightshirts and foul language in the presence of gently bred young women. He cleared his throat, determined to keep their relationship on a professional footing. "Come to my study on the morrow, Amelia. We can discuss your plans for the boys."

She nodded. "As you wish, Your Grace. But you should call me Miss Saxton. Otherwise..."

"Very well," he agreed. "Goodnight, Miss Saxton."

~

Amelia paused before tapping on the door of the boys' bedchamber. She considered stopping by her own room to retrieve a fan, but not everything had been unpacked. With any luck, the lads wouldn't notice she was flustered and overheated. In the course of the morrow's discussions, she might stipulate a preference to eat her meals with the servants. Dining every day with Warrick Farrell had the potential to turn her into a seething mass of wanton feelings. The orphans were astute and would quickly notice something was up.

She had to stiffen her backbone and concentrate on the reason she'd come to Derbyshire. There was absolutely nothing to be gained from pining for what could never be.

She stepped back when the door opened abruptly and Carlos appeared.

"*Señorita*," he said, executing an exaggerated bow. She nodded and proceeded into the chamber, somewhat relieved when he closed the door and left. He was a difficult person to figure out.

The boys were all in their beds. Five smiling faces swept away her doubts. She would do her best to prepare them for a good life. That was the important task ahead of her. She went to each bed in turn, tucked in the sheets and pecked a kiss on the occupant's forehead. "Sleep well," she said as she tiptoed out of the chamber.

She unpacked a few personal items before

undressing and donning her nightgown. Having at last secured the kind of position she'd always hoped for, she anticipated a good night's sleep. The predatory Knowsley had spoiled her first opportunity. She was confident Warrick Farrell was an honorable man who would never encroach—no matter how much she might want him to.

~

QUITE SURE HE'D have trouble sleeping knowing Amelia Saxton was abed in a chamber on the same floor as his own, Warrick retired to the library, poured himself a brandy and settled into a chair before the fire. Even sipping slowly didn't lessen the swelling at his groin brought on by Amelia's blush. He spread his legs and used his hand to rearrange things more comfortably.

In the slums, a man never thought twice about easing pressure in the male equipment area. God help him, he'd almost done what came naturally during the evening meal. The lads would have had a fine time jesting about that lapse. He was supposed to be setting a good example.

Amelia might have swooned. On second thoughts, though, he doubted it. Right from the outset of his new life, she'd been the one person who'd accepted him immediately, despite his rough edges. Or perhaps because of them?

That thought necessitated another adjustment. He ought to retire and seek relief in his chamber, though

Carlos was probably laying out the nightshirt Warrick had told him a thousand times he didn't care to wear.

He closed his eyes. Forty winks, then he'd make his way upstairs.

∽

AMELIA REASONED it was to be expected that sleep would prove elusive in a strange bed. She was overtired after the journey. Fretting about the morrow's meeting with the duke had nothing to do with her restlessness.

She had packed several books in her luggage, but they consisted mostly of adventure tales suitable for boys. What she needed was a novel to send her to sleep, otherwise she feared she'd be tossing and turning all night.

During a brief tour of the downstairs rooms, she'd poked her head into what looked like a well-stocked library. There was one main staircase which she could easily navigate in the dark.

The house was quiet. Only the distant hoot of an owl broke the silence. Assuming everyone was abed, she donned the wrapper she'd left at the foot of the bed, gave up on locating her slippers and ventured into the hallway barefoot.

It took a few minutes for her eyes to adjust to the utter darkness. Holding her breath, she gripped the banister and took the stairs one at a time.

Having reached the lower floor safely, she recalled the library was one of only two rooms with a fireplace, which explained the faint glow under the door. Hopefully, there would be enough light to see the book titles on the shelves.

Praying the door didn't creak, she opened it slowly, stole inside and closed it quickly.

A fire-screen had been placed around the hearty flames still burning in the hearth. Reassured there was nothing to worry about, she tiptoed to the shelves and began her search.

Engrossed in peering at the spines on the second shelf she'd perused, she froze when she heard a noise that sounded remarkably like soft snoring.

Gooseflesh marched across her nape when she turned slowly and saw Warrick sprawled in a chair.

The proper thing to do would be to flee before he awoke, but she couldn't seem to take her eyes off long legs stretched out before the fire. The butterflies fluttering in her stomach turned into a mass winged migration when she realized his hand rested atop...

Oh, Lord!

Unlike her, he looked perfectly relaxed. A day on the road had resulted in the beginnings of a dark mustache and beard. She could no longer deny that she loved this pirate rogue, but he'd be mortified if he woke and realized she'd seen him in such an intimate pose.

She had no brothers. She'd changed Avery's nappies, but the genitalia of an adult male were a complete mystery to her. Telling herself she simply had an inquiring mind, she tried desperately to resist the urge to know what lay beneath his long fingers. Without warning, dark lashes fluttered and he opened his eyes.

Her throat tightened and she stopped breathing

when he stretched his arms above his head, revealing a distinct bulge where his hand had been.

He sat bolt upright when he finally saw her. She stared into startled green eyes for what felt like an eternity before she fled.

LONG RANGE PLANS

Awaiting Amelia's arrival for their scheduled meeting, Warrick paced in the study where his father's presence lingered. After last night's fiasco in the library, he doubted he'd ever live up to his late sire's expectations.

When he'd realized Amelia had caught him with his hand on his privates, his first instinct was to prevent her from leaving the library.

And say what? *Sorry, I'm an uncouth fellow.*

She probably thought so anyway.

He could still explain. *My cock grew hard thinking of you and I sought to ease the ache.*

Nothing like making things worse. She was an innocent who'd likely never heard the word *cock* and would have no inkling what happened when a man wanted a woman.

When she didn't appear in the breakfast nook, Wilson informed him she'd ordered trays sent to the boys' chamber. He'd welcomed the reprieve. Carlos had refused to shave him, insisting he'd look more like a Spanish pirate if he let his beard grow. After a sleepless night, he hadn't the energy to argue, though the pirate logic was lost on him and the itching was driving him mad.

The irony was he'd rarely shaved in Hull. He knew the itching would eventually cease, but the irritation underlined how pampered he'd become.

However, Amelia was due to arrive any moment, and he still didn't know what he should say. Perhaps it was best to simply act as though the incident had never happened.

But it had and, if he were honest with himself, he didn't regret it. Amelia had been aroused. He'd seen it in those wide eyes, caught a whiff of it when she scurried by him to make her escape—in bare feet!

"You're a fool," he said aloud as his cock swelled. "That just compounds the problem."

A light tap at the door heralded her arrival. "Come in," he croaked from his dry throat as he slipped into the chair behind the desk.

∼

AN HOUR SPENT EATING breakfast with the orphans had driven thoughts of the previous night's embarrassing incident from the forefront of Amelia's mind. She'd wanted to know more about the boys' lives in Hull before she met with Warrick to discuss her plans.

What she'd learned about their difficult childhoods stiffened her resolve to think only of her charges. She entered the study, determined not to mention last night. "I've a better understanding of what's needed," she began, noticing he hadn't shaved. About to tell him she found the beginnings of a neatly trimmed beard and mustache appealing, she cleared her throat and dragged her thoughts back to what was important. "They are all motherless, so it's no wonder they respond to feminine affection."

"They are males after all," Warrick replied with a hint of a smile. "Please be seated."

She filled her lungs as she sat across the desk from him. Clearly, he wasn't going to make this easy. "They are also fatherless, so we must meet their need for masculine guidance. It would be beneficial, for example, if one or two of the footmen could accompany us on rambles through the dales."

"I'd enjoy coming along on those walks," he said. "I am their guardian and I want to become more familiar with this area."

She tried frantically to reorganize her thoughts. "Yes, of course. Also, Philip generously gave me a few pieces of laboratory equipment and some suggestions for simple experiments."

"I'd be very interested in that," he replied.

Of course he would. Too late, she remembered his fascination with the laboratory at Wentworth.

She adopted her best governess voice. "In addition, we must concentrate on the usual skills—reading, writing, arithmetic."

She regretted the words when the color drained from his face. She'd hit on his sore spot. He too needed to learn the basics and she was the only person who could help him. He might be embarrassed enough to dismiss her, but she forged ahead. "I know you cannot read or write, Your Grace. I will exercise the utmost discretion and gladly assist you to overcome this obstacle."

∽

A LEAD BALL of humiliation lodged in Warrick's gut. Not only had Amelia seen him at his bestial worst, she'd guessed correctly that he was illiterate. He could deny her assertion, but why lie?

Hope gradually surfaced. Who better than Amelia Saxton to lift him out of ignorance? She understood his lack of education and didn't judge him for it. He could be bullheaded and refuse her help, or he could welcome it. "I appreciate your offer," he said, biting back the urge to suggest private evening lessons, perhaps in the library.

No!

His determination to keep his distance had flown out the window and he'd insinuated himself into all her plans for the curriculum.

Falling back on something she'd said earlier, he cautioned, "Just one thing you should be aware of. The boys are not all fatherless."

Her eyes widened. "Oh?"

"Kenny ran to me when his drunken father flogged him to within an inch of his life. It wasn't the first time he'd beaten the boy in a gin-fueled rage."

Again, he'd spoken of cruel things a genteel young woman should know nothing about.

"What?" she shrieked indignantly, launching herself out of the chair. "Then, he's well rid of the brute."

Thank goodness he hadn't mentioned the weeks of tending Kenny's lacerated flesh and the months of rocking him in his arms when the nightmares refused to leave the boy in peace. "Well, his father threatened several times to get him back, but I managed to thwart him."

He deemed it preferable not to elaborate on exactly how he'd *thwarted* Joss Watkins with his fists.

Tears welled in her eyes. "It's a good thing Kenny is now far away from his father's clutches," she said. "He didn't mention any of this to me."

"I'm not surprised. He's terrified of the bugger."

He expected she'd be shocked by his lapse into the vocabulary of the streets. Instead, she smiled and said, "I think *bugger* is the perfect word for such a coward."

THE TRIUMVIRATE

eeling more optimistic after her unladylike quip banished the uncertainty from Warrick's handsome face, Amelia regained her seat and suggested they tackle his education in two ways. "The boys won't think it strange if you sit in on their lessons. In fact, they'll appreciate that you are taking an interest in their progress. It will be up to you to pay close attention."

"I promise to do so, Miss Saxton," he replied with mock seriousness.

The pirate rogue was toying with her. Surely he too realized that they had no future together? Perhaps flirting came naturally to the male of the species. Her mother had often told her it was the pursuit that motivated men. The poor creatures were slaves to their base desires. She shuddered as the memory of Knowsley's lechery intruded.

If Warrick was incapable of maintaining a professional demeanor, then she would set the tone. "Secondly, you'll need private lessons. I propose we conduct them early in the morning, perhaps somewhere we won't be disturbed. It wouldn't be entirely proper to be discovered alone together."

He narrowed his eyes. "We're alone together now."

"True, but Wilson might interrupt at any moment and..."

As if to bear out her prediction, the butler appeared in the doorway after tapping lightly. "Messrs. Mawdsley, Mawdsley and Mawdsley are waiting to see you, Your Grace. I put the legal gentlemen in the drawing room."

"Show them in," Warrick replied without hesitation.

Panic tightened Amelia's throat as the butler left. "No, that won't do, Your Grace. They cannot see me here."

"Wilson saw us alone. I'm sure several of the servants know of our meeting."

"You have much to learn about the ways of the nobility," she replied, heading for the door. "Solicitors are not servants. They will quickly spread word of our indiscretion."

"We're not committing an indiscretion, Miss Saxton," he replied coldly. "You are governess to my young charges and it seems perfectly natural for us to hold meetings."

Her spirits fell. Perhaps she'd imagined he was flirting.

Before she could regain her equilibrium and point out the error of his assumption, he continued. "Besides, they've come for the legal papers. I'd like you to be here when I hand them over. Just in case."

"They'll consider it highly irregular."

"Let them," he replied as Wilson ushered the visitors into the study.

※

Warrick rose to greet the Mawdsleys. He knew full well he'd placed Amelia in a difficult position. The newly minted Duke of Beaufort chastised himself for it. Warrick Farrell, denizen of the slums, relished her fierce blush and didn't care a whit for the aristocratic nonsense of keeping up appearances.

The solicitors tried hard to mask their disdain when he introduced Amelia as the boys' governess. He'd wager none of the three had ever been married. They declined to be seated and, instead, stood waiting, clearly expecting her to leave.

"Miss Saxton and I were discussing matters of curriculum," he said, handing the legal portfolio to the eldest brother. "I assume you wish to peruse these duly signed and sealed documents. That should only take a few minutes then the governess and I can get on with our planning."

They reminded him of vultures picking over a carcass as they removed pince-nez, affixed monocles and examined every page, their shoulders hunched. His thinly veiled dismissal had offended them, but they only muttered their discontent. No doubt they would mention his rudeness in their accounts of the meeting. Let them characterize him as just another arrogant aristocrat. Perhaps then Amelia's presence wouldn't take center stage.

That hope flew away like a startled bird when she spoke. "Excuse me, Your Grace," she said politely. "Have you discussed with these gentlemen the importance of having your guardianship of the boys legally confirmed?"

William Mawdsley's eyes widened. Dislodged from the folds of his eye socket, the monocle suddenly dangled from its black ribbon. "I don't see..."

"Miss Saxton makes a very good point," Warrick said. "I'll provide a list of names and circumstances if you'd be good enough to look into it."

The trio stared at him as if he'd spoken in Greek. Archibald Mawdsley recovered first. "Of course, Your Grace. We'll pursue legal guardianship once we receive the information. The documents of succession appear to be in order."

"I appreciate it, gentlemen," he replied, uttering a silent prayer of thanks to Philip Fortescue. "Wilson will see you out."

Once the click of the front door closing assured him the triumvirate had left the premises, Warrick raised an eyebrow.

"You handled that very well, Your Grace," Amelia said, her eyes bright.

"And you managed to stifle the urge to giggle, Miss Saxton," he replied with a broad grin.

That was all it took to release the laughter bubbling inside them.

AMELIA LAUGHED SO HARD she could scarcely catch her breath. Then the hiccups began, which Warrick evidently found even more amusing.

"I think," she managed at last, "that you will make a perfect duke."

Sobering, he shook his head.

"Truly," she insisted. "You bring a sort of rough bravado that will stand you in good stead. You know how to think on your feet."

"Surviving in the slums depended on it," he replied.

"So, you see, your previous life is actually an asset. Use it to your advantage."

She was relieved to see his smile return. "I never thought of it that way."

"You have a good heart, which is another thing in your favor. You make decisions with the welfare of others in mind."

"I'm not the selfless person you think I am, Amelia," he replied, all trace of humor gone. "Otherwise, I wouldn't have asked you to come here."

"I know that," she admitted. "And I was too selfish to refuse."

RISE ABOVE IT

Amelia recommended that Warrick's education begin subtly. Thus, he attended a writing lesson in the schoolroom his father had financed and equipped with the necessities of a good education. There, he watched her write the letters of the alphabet on a large slate attached to the wall. The lads assured her they already knew the letters, but she nevertheless had them read the whole alphabet aloud five times. Warrick was grateful. The repetition was for his benefit.

Amelia then encouraged each boy to write his name on his individual slate.

This was all Greek to Warrick, but they had no trouble writing their names. They flushed with pleasure when he congratulated them. They couldn't know how proud he truly was. They were already better equipped for a new life than he was.

However, he grew increasingly nervous. His was a long name and he doubted he'd remember all the necessary letters and the sounds associated with them once he was alone in his study. He envied the ease of youth to learn new things.

To his relief, Amelia made it easier. "Did you know," she asked, "that your guardian, His Grace, must use only his title when he signs documents?"

"You mean he writes just Beaufort?" Kenny asked.

"Well done, Mr. Watkins. Would anyone like to volunteer to print that name on the slate?"

Eddie almost leaped from his seat and took the chalk from her hand. "That's easy, Miss Saxton."

The chalk squeaked on the dark surface as Eddie wrote *Bofort*. Bestowing a superior grin on the others, he dusted off his hands and regained his seat.

Warrick peered at the slate, committing the symbols to memory.

"Good try, Mr. Powell," Miss Saxton said, erasing Eddie's effort with a damp cloth. "Unfortunately, English is not always written the way it sounds. Beaufort comes from the French language, so it's spelled thusly."

On the slate, she printed *BEAUFORT*.

Warrick's spirits lifted. He recognized the word he'd written on the documents with Philip's help.

His pride soared when Amelia announced, "As the Duke of Beaufort's wards, you'll need to learn how to spell the title. Repeat after me, B, E, A, U, F, O, R, T."

She had them repeat the exercise. Warrick mouthed the spelling along with them.

When he regained his study shortly thereafter, he was able to write *Beaufort* over and over. The heavy burden of ignorance lifted from his shoulders. He wasn't stupid. He could learn and, by God, he would—with Amelia's help.

~

Amelia and the boys spent the early part of the afternoon setting up the retort stands, test tubes and flasks Philip had given her. She decided against including the spirit lamps for the moment. She wanted to instill a love for science but couldn't risk burning the manor down.

Her charges insisted upon eating luncheon in the schoolroom when she told them about her plans for the afternoon. They wanted to get on with setting up a laboratory and their enthusiasm was gratifying.

She had a tray brought for herself as well, although she was anxious to find out Warrick's thoughts about the writing lesson. She was smugly pleased with the surreptitious way she'd taught him to write his title. But the proof was in the pudding, as the saying went.

He joined them as the last piece of equipment was put in place. The joy on his face spoke volumes. Elation soared as she bade the boys greet their guardian.

"Good afternoon, Your Grace," they dutifully intoned.

"Good afternoon, gentlemen," he replied. "Since you have learned how to spell my title, I suggest you use it instead of Your Grace."

Amelia set the example. "Good afternoon, Beaufort."

"Good afternoon, Beaufort," they echoed.

"We've made a lavatory," Tim announced.

The rest laughed, but Amelia was relieved they didn't poke fun at Tim.

"Laboratory," Kenny corrected.

"So I see," Warrick replied.

"We don't 'ave one of them tubes you look into, though," Charlie complained. "Mecks tiny things look bigger."

"You mean a microscope," Warrick replied. "Well, if you lads make progress with your studies, we'll try to obtain one."

Amelia swallowed the lump in her throat. One would think from the joy on their faces he'd promised them a year's supply of gobstoppers. "I think you've worked hard enough for today," she said. "You're free to play cricket in the rear courtyard until Carlos sends word it's time to prepare for dinner."

All interest in science fled as they scarpered from the schoolroom.

Smiling broadly, Warrick produced a piece of paper from his inside pocket and presented it to her.

Tears welled. He'd written his title over and over, each version showing a little more confidence. She wanted to kiss him, but had to make do with teasing. "There's just one problem, Beaufort."

"Oh?" he replied with a cautious frown.

"I can read this perfectly. A duke's signature should be impossible to decipher."

His shoulders relaxed. "I know. Philip taught me that's where all the flourishes and squiggly lines come in. I can manage those."

"I've put this off," Warrick told Amelia as he handed over a thick envelope. "A courier delivered a packet in my absence. It was sitting on my desk. I suspect it's an invitation."

Amelia's face paled as she accepted the letter. "The royal crest. The coronation."

"That's what I thought. I suppose peers are expected to attend, but..."

"You'll have to go," she declared. "It's an honor."

"My lack of education will become obvious."

"We have some time to work on remedying that. When is the ceremony?"

"Open it and see," he said with a shrug.

"It's to take place on July 19th," she read, running her fingers over the embossed invitation. "It's signed by the Deputy Earl Marshal, Lord Howard and countersigned by the Duke of Wellington. It admits you to a seat in the Lord Steward's box in the Poet's Corner of Westminster Abbey."

His gut clenched. "I'll be a laughing stock."

"No," she replied vehemently. "Alex and Philip will both be there. You know you can rely on them. You may not have the background of other peers of the realm, but I've already pointed out that isn't necessarily a handicap."

The knot in his belly loosened. He wished he could take her in his arms and soak up the confidence she had in him. "You have too much faith in me," he sighed.

"No. You must have faith in yourself, just as your father did. You'll be representing him."

She was right. He should be proud to attend. "I wish you could come with me," he said.

She shook her head. "A nobody like me would never be invited to such an important event."

Her words saddened him. It was more than likely both her sisters would attend with their ducal husbands. Eliza and Jenny Saxton were outstanding examples of commoners who'd married above their station and fitted right into their new roles.

As if divining his thoughts, she said, "You and I both know my sisters are well-respected duchesses, but there are still many among the peerage who will cut them because of their birth. They rise above it, as you must."

Warrick's admiration for this remarkable woman grew. If it weren't for his father's insistence on the importance of marrying a titled heiress, he would offer for Amelia.

PROGRESS

Modifying writing lessons in order to teach Warrick was relatively easy. The boys willingly wrote his surname on their slates then vied for turns to show off their attempts. He announced he would have to take all the slates to his study to determine which was the neatest.

They repeated the performance with his first name, then progressed on to Miss Saxton, Derbyshire and Cavendish Manor. There was a lot of eye-rolling when it came to an explanation of the different sounds the vowels could make. The boys deemed the notion of silent *e* completely ridiculous.

Practicing the sound made by combining *s* and *h* caused a lot of hilarity as they tried to out-shush each other.

They were left with only a handful of letters unaccounted for. "Who can tell me which letters we haven't included in our lessons?" she asked.

Kenny had no trouble peeling off G, J, P, Q and Z.

The lads willingly called out words they thought used the extra letters and she wrote them on the slate.

It was clear that Kenny was a bright boy who learned quickly. Amelia shuddered to think what might have become of him had it not been for Warrick. He'd probably be dead.

Satisfied she'd done her best to teach all her pupils the letters of the alphabet, she was thrilled when Warrick assured her privately he could write the words they'd practiced. He was beginning to understand how the sounds fit together to make words. It pleased her to no end to know he had practiced writing *Miss Saxton*. Her heart nigh on burst when he surreptitiously passed her a piece of paper on which he'd printed AMELEA.

~

WARRICK BECAME ENGROSSED in Amelia's readings from a book called *Swiss Family Robinson*. The boys groaned when she came to the end of a chapter, begging to know what came next. However, it wasn't simply the story that kept Warrick's attention. He loved the sound of her voice and the expressive way she told the tale. He longed for a day when he too could narrate a gripping story to the lads.

She asked questions after each reading, thus cleverly ascertaining who had really listened. Completely ignoring shouted answers, she managed to train them to raise a hand if they wished to be acknowledged.

She usually chose the boy with the best posture at his desk. Soon, no one slouched. Equally greedy to be in her

UNCOUTH DUKE

good graces, Warrick found himself squaring his shoulders and straightening his spine.

After each lesson, she allowed him to borrow her copy of the book. He pored over the text she'd read, eventually able to recognize some of the meaning in the symbols. He tried to read some of the books in his father's library, frustrated with his lack of success until Amelia found an illustrated copy of *Gulliver's Travels* for him. Ostensibly, the daily discussions in his study were regarding curriculum and the boys' progress. In fact, she spent the time explaining the gist of each forthcoming chapter then left him to puzzle out the words on the pages.

His confidence in his ability to learn grew when the words made sense. Amelia Saxton wasn't simply preparing his charges for a better life. She'd shown Warrick himself that he had the intelligence to survive and prosper as a duke. He could never repay her.

That notion saddened him. It was obvious she cared for him more than she should. Eventually, they would have to part. She wouldn't be the only one with a broken heart when that day came. He could no longer deny he didn't simply admire and respect Amelia. He'd loved her from the moment they met.

~

AMELIA WELL REMEMBERED her late father's fondness for *Gulliver's Travels.* However, she had never really enjoyed the book until Warrick took so much obvious pleasure from the story.

He nodded his understanding of Swift's clever satire when she explained the hidden significance of the Lilliputians' small stature. "Their miniature size represents the cultural differences of the civilizations that England encountered in the course of its expansion in the seventeen hundreds."

"And the tiniest race is the vainest," he replied. "Just like some small-minded people are excessively proud."

"Exactly," she agreed, amazed at the depth of his perception. She wondered if he too was thinking of her mother then chastised herself for the unkind thought.

"The Lilliputians waged war against their neighbors because they cracked their eggs in a different way. My father explained that Swift was poking fun at England's conflicts with France—a series of brutal wars over meaningless and arbitrary disagreements."

He laughed heartily when Gulliver was eventually convicted of treason for urinating on a fire in the royal palace. "It doesn't matter he put the fire out," he chuckled.

She loved to see him happy and pleased with his progress.

Their discussions proved to Amelia that Warrick had an agile mind. He fully understood Swift's belief that size, power, and individual rank were all relative.

It was a bittersweet realization. Not only did he have the makings of a good duke, he would be a wonderful life partner for some lucky woman.

During the day, she relied on steely resolve to hide her heartbreak. Tears flowed into her pillow every night.

VISITORS

Reluctant to participate in preparations for his departure for London, Warrick nevertheless accepted he had no choice. His failure to attend the coronation would be brought to the new king's attention, thus denigrating the reputation of the Beaufort dukedom.

His biggest concern was leaving Amelia and the boys. Despite her insistence they would be too busy to notice his absence, her constant frown let him know she dreaded his departure.

The problem was alleviated somewhat by a letter addressed to him from Amelia's brother-in-law. Wanting to be certain he fully understood the contents, he invited her to the study.

After perusing the missive, she told him, "Alex suggests he and Philip come to Cavendish and the three of you travel to London together. They've secured accommodation."

His spirits lifted. "Good idea. My business manager is having trouble finding a place in the city. It seems everyone and his dog will be in London then."

She grinned as she read further. "Apparently, Eliza and Jenny prefer not to attend the coronation. They'd rather spend a few days here with me."

Her obvious joy at the news lightened the dread of his impending departure. "Will they bring their little ones?" he asked.

"Yes, and Mama insists on coming too."

He wasn't sure if she was happy about the prospect of her mother's visit, but it was a relief she'd be surrounded by family while he was away.

～

Hugging her sisters after they alit from the Harrowby and Wentworth coaches three days later, Amelia let the tears flow. "I didn't realize how much I've missed all of you," she confessed.

Her mother harrumphed. "It's not *that* long since you were at Wentworth."

Feeling guilty that she and her sisters had left their mother out of the joyful reunion, Amelia couldn't fault her mother's pout.

"Don't feel badly," Eliza whispered close to Amelia's ear. "Mama started out in our carriage and played the role of doting grandmama for the first hour. I admit we were cramped, and there was more room in the Wentworth vehicle. Mama insisted on changing to Jenny's carriage, but claimed it was because of the dog. Thank goodness Nanny Brown then switched to be with me."

Nodding sympathetically, Amelia knelt and opened her arms to her nephews.

Sax came willingly. "Aunty Amelia," he declared.

"You've grown so much," she replied.

"Mama says I'll be taller than Papa when I grow up."

"I think she's right."

Even bigger than the last time she'd seen him, Brutus nuzzled his way into the embrace.

Clinging to Nanny Brown's skirts, Avery and Jenny's Rowland watched, clearly wary. Living in a different county meant these boys did not remember her. However, Warrick and the lads had also come to the forecourt to welcome everyone. She didn't want them to think she had regrets about moving to Derbyshire.

Sax saved the day. "Don't be scared. She's our Aunt," he announced.

Tail wagging furiously, Brutus barked a confirmation.

Apparently reassured, Avery and Rowland allowed her to embrace them.

"You're so big," she exclaimed.

"You have hugs for everyone but me," her mother whined. "And I see the miscreants from Hull are still here."

Before Amelia could reply, Warrick stepped forward. "Lady Penelope," he said as he bowed at the waist and took hold of her hand. "Welcome to Cavendish Manor."

"Thank you, Your Grace," she replied, an uncharacteristic blush reddening her cheeks when he brushed a kiss on her knuckles.

"He's learned diplomacy," Jenny whispered to Amelia.

"He's a quick study," she replied hoarsely.

Jenny eyed her curiously, obviously hearing the longing Amelia had tried to suppress.

She was spared an inquisition by the arrival on horseback of her brothers-in-law.

"Our husbands wisely chose not to travel with the menagerie," Eliza explained. "There wasn't room anyway."

Warrick hurried to welcome his fellow dukes as they dismounted. Despite terrible injuries suffered at Waterloo, Alex Harcourt was still an imposing figure of a man. His wife's expertise in Swedish exercise and massage had helped him regain most of his mobility. The patch covering his glass eye only added to his allure.

Any woman would be attracted to Philip Fortescue's noble bearing, athletic grace, and ready smile.

Yet, in Amelia's opinion, Warrick Farrell was the equal of her brothers-in-law in every way.

~

WARRICK HADN'T KNOWN his dining room table could be extended to accommodate everyone—and he apparently owned enough matching chairs. He whispered his thanks to Wilson as he escorted Lady Penelope to a seat next to his own.

"My pleasure, Your Grace," the butler replied. "It's a delight to have the house full again."

It was true that the presence of little ones made Cavendish Manor seem more like a home, although he thought of the urchins as his brood—and Amelia the mother hen!

He supposed his father's house had once been full of life—until tragedy struck the Hastings family. When the duchess and her son were killed in a carriage accident, Cavendish Manor must have felt like a tomb to the grief-stricken Duke of Beaufort.

One day, Warrick would find a suitable wife and raise his own family here. He looked forward to fathering children, something he'd never considered in his previous life. He'd lavish love on them and make sure they had all the advantages wealth could bring. He fancied his sons would take after him. His daughters all had Amelia's chestnut brown hair and hazel eyes, no matter how hard he tried to will away the vision.

It was imperative he find his heiress soon, before it became impossible to forget Amelia Saxton. The festivities in London might provide an opportunity to meet suitable women. The prospect held no appeal as he watched Amelia bask in the pleasure of her family's warmth. The Harcourts and Fortescues were his friends, but he craved more. He wanted to be an integral part of this intimate group—to belong.

The boys behaved like perfect gentlemen, to the degree that even Lady Penelope remarked on it. He sensed it wasn't simply because Amelia expected it of them. They now expected it of themselves. She'd wrought a miracle in a short period of time. However, if he didn't free himself of his preoccupation with her soon, he never would.

∽

Crouched behind a row of cedars lining the avenue leading to Cavendish Manor, Joss Watkins snarled when curtains were drawn, blocking his view of a brightly lit room full of people.

"Enjoyin' a fancy meal my lad is," he growled. "Whilst my belly rumbles."

"Nowt to eat since yestermorn," Freddie Entwistle said. "Then only the loaf we nicked."

Joss was sick and tired of Freddie's whining that had started the minute they'd left Hull. He'd thought it wise to bring an accomplice to aid in retrieving his ungrateful, runaway son. After a week trudging along dusty roads, he now understood the reason for the nickname by which Freddie was universally known. He truly did put one in mind of a ferret. "Shut yer yap," he ordered.

"S'pose they ask if we're sperienced gardners?"

"We lie," Joss replied, sorely tempted to backhand the twit so hard he might never wake up. "Workin' int' grounds will put us near Kenny."

"Then we grab 'im and go," Freddie said.

"Nay," Joss replied. "I owe yon Farrell a beatin' he won't soon forget."

"Who'da thunk it? Warrick Farrell a duke," Freddie said.

Joss clenched his jaw. At first, he hadn't believed the

rumors. Farrell seemed to have disappeared, and Kenny with him. It had taken months to track down where they'd gone. But he'd found them. Soon, his worthless son would be back in his hands. Kenny Watkins belonged in Hull, thieving for his Da, not in some bleeding mansion miles away.

DEPARTURE

S tanding in the forecourt with her family and the urchins, Amelia tried to put on a brave face, but even her charges noted her distress.

"Nay worries, Miss Saxton," Kenny assured her. "Warrick'll be back before tha kens he's gone."

The governess in her itched to point out he shouldn't be using his guardian's given name and the temptation to correct his use of *tha* instead of *you* was powerful. However, she doubted anything coherent would emerge from her parched throat.

"Aye," Eddie added, thrusting out his chest. "Tha's allays got us to protec' thee."

She'd dreaded Warrick's departure but couldn't credit there was anything to fear at Cavendish.

Alex's little Avery wailed, his head on his father's shoulder.

His hand curled into the dog's collar, his brother Sax stood to attention like a tin soldier, clearly trying not to show his upset that his Papa was leaving.

Eliza too struggled with tears as she pried Avery back into her arms.

Alex embraced his family, rubbed the wolfhound's ears and boarded the carriage as quickly as his limp allowed.

Not to be outdone, Jenny's son screamed, holding out his little arms for his Papa. Philip kissed Rowland's forehead. "We'll be back in a few days," he assured his wife before joining Alex.

Amelia's consternation grew as Warrick shook hands with each of the lads. Soon, it would be her turn.

"Miss Saxton," he said. "I'll miss you."

And with that, he turned away and boarded the carriage.

"I'll miss you, too," she whispered as the conveyance picked up speed, carrying the man she loved to London where he would meet his future wife.

∼

THE THREE DUKES spent the first night in a comfortable inn on the outskirts of Northampton. Philip had apparently made the arrangements beforehand. Warrick was shown to a spacious room which boasted its own facilities. Given the rutted conditions of the roads, there hadn't been much opportunity for meaningful conversation during the journey. Warrick hoped to remedy that when he, Alex and Philip met for an evening meal.

He shouldn't have been surprised when the innkeeper ushered him to a private dining room downstairs.

His fellow dukes stood to greet him with a handshake. He liked the polite gesture although it seemed silly after they'd spent hours together in the carriage.

"So," Philip began. "Let's plan our strategy."

Warrick chuckled. Alex and Philip had both been officers in the British army and old habits apparently died hard.

"I suppose we'll be expected to attend the various balls, musicales, soirées, etcetera, etcetera," Alex said.

"Balls?" Warrick asked.

"George will probably host the biggest one at Carlton House," Philip explained.

Alex nodded. "But there'll be many noble families who want to show their support of the king. At least I won't be expected to dance."

"Whereas Warrick and I will have to show willing," Philip said. "Do you know how to dance?"

"My father insisted I take lessons in the most popular dances," Warrick replied. "But I've never actually danced with a partner."

"I'm surprised Amelia didn't prepare you for the waltz," Alex remarked. "She's not one to leave any stone unturned."

Warrick knew full well why Amelia hadn't suggested they waltz together and he was grateful for it.

"These balls will provide the perfect opportunity for you to meet your future wife," Philip said.

Warrick nodded, not certain what to make of the sudden intense scrutiny of his fellow dukes.

Alex and Philip's sons fretted after their fathers' departure. Even Sax's usual good humor was nowhere in evidence and Brutus whimpered constantly. Curiously enough, it was the lads from Hull who succeeded in distracting the little ones from their upset. After seeking Amelia's permission to skip their lessons, they took the three ducal sons to the stables and then toured the grounds around the house.

Avery and Rowland held hands with Eddie and Kenny, little legs working hard to keep up with their unexpected champions. Sax followed along as if he didn't care, but soon hurried to catch up and be part of the group.

"I can't credit you're allowing those ruffians to take my grandsons off to who knows where," Lady Penelope declared.

"They aren't ruffians," Amelia retorted.

"Their behavior is markedly improved," Jenny said. "It's good for Rowland to have other boys to play with."

"And soon he'll have a baby brother or sister," Eliza said, patting Jenny's expanding waist.

Amelia embraced Jenny. "I'm thrilled for you and Philip," she said.

"And you must congratulate Eliza too," her sister replied.

Amelia eyed her elder sister. "You're expecting again?"

Eliza nodded, earning a fierce embrace from both sisters.

"Of course, no one thinks to inform me," Lady Penelope muttered, before flouncing off into the house.

"I feel left out too," Amelia complained. "You didn't share your happy news with me."

In truth, her sadness had more to do with jealousy. Her sisters had married men they loved and started families. She was destined to remain a spinster all her life. If she couldn't have Warrick Farrell, she wasn't willing to consider marrying anyone else.

∼

"S'pose we'll just 'ave to nab yer brat and be gone," Freddie said as he and Joss watched the carriage carry Warrick Farrell away from Cavendish Manor.

"Tha thinks I've come all this distance and slept rough just to get me 'ands on Kenny?" Joss replied. "Nay, Farrell will be back."

"But when?" Freddie whined.

"'Ow should I know? If we wait too long, there's allays the little kiddies."

"Nay," Freddie replied, making a choking sound as he hoisted himself with an imaginary rope. "Kidnappers get 'ung."

Freddie was right, but Joss had to exact his revenge somehow. Taking back his son wasn't enough. He'd have to come up with a good plan, but first things first. "We'll find yon servants' door and sign on as gardners."

He cuffed Freddie's ear when the ferret whined about knowing nowt about gardening.

THIS AND THAT

The Harrowby carriage came to a halt in front of an impressive townhouse in an area of London far removed from the bustling streets and congested districts they'd driven through. Hull was a fair sized city with some mighty fine residential neighborhoods, but Warrick had never seen anything like this neighborhood. "We're not far from Westminster," Philip explained, "And our former commanding officer in the army was only too pleased to host us and a few other comrades in arms."

Warrick's spirits fell. He knew of many dockworkers from Hull who'd volunteered to fight the French and never returned. He'd avoided enlisting, primarily because he didn't want to be cannon fodder for aristocratic officers. In this company of military men, he'd be deemed a coward.

"It's unavoidable you'll hear tales of the campaigns," Alex said. "Old soldiers can't talk about anything else!"

"And the stories get more and more exaggerated with

each retelling," Philip quipped as the door was opened by their driver.

"Just don't bring up my misadventure," Alex said to Philip.

"But I like boasting that I saved your miserable hide," his friend replied with a wink.

Warrick knew of the special bond that existed between the two dukes. They'd been friends since Eton, and Philip had indeed saved Alex's life at Waterloo. It was thus all the more remarkable that the chums had taken Warrick under their wing and offered to guide him through the early stages of his new life. They were noble men in the true sense of the word—men to emulate. His background argued against becoming their equal, but he was determined to make every effort.

∼

PHILIP ALWAYS ENJOYED GETTING TOGETHER with former comrades and rehashing war stories. Knowing other men had experienced the same horrors made the nightmarish memories easier to bear. It had been years since he'd dragged Alex from beneath a dying horse, yet it felt like only yesterday.

Knowing Alex didn't like to dwell on the tale of the catastrophe that befell him at Waterloo, Philip deliberately made light of his heroism when another officer brought it up.

He also steered the conversation away from Warrick when some chaps questioned why he hadn't joined the army. They assumed a duke would have bought his son a commission. To his credit, Warrick made no excuses. "I wasn't recognized as the son of a duke in those days," he said.

This resulted in the exchange of a few curious glances, but no one pursued the matter.

When the war stories dried up, the talk turned inevitably to women—in particular to eligible misses the unmarried men hoped to meet at the various functions held in conjunction with the coronation.

"You have competition, my friend," Philip quipped to Warrick.

"I suppose," came the unenthusiastic reply.

"Don't worry. With your looks and a wealthy dukedom to offer, you'll charm some titled lady."

As the color drained from Warrick's face, Philip knew Alex had the right of it when he claimed the Duke of Beaufort was enamored of Amelia Saxton.

∽

IN THE FIELD behind Cavendish Manor, Jenny, Amelia and their mother sat in deckchairs watching Saxton and Brutus play cricket with the lads. Sound asleep, Rowland lay sprawled atop his mother's swollen stomach. Jenny looked askance at her sister. "It's obvious you're pining for Beaufort," she said.

Amelia bristled. "Hush," she replied. "Someone might hear."

"The lads are too engrossed in their game, and Sax is obviously enjoying their attention."

"That's the only problem with being the son of a

duke," Eliza added as she joined them. "He has no one his own age to play with."

"Better no playmates than those ruffians," Lady Penelope huffed.

"Avery got down all right?" Amelia asked, ignoring her mother's grumble.

"Sleeping soundly with Nanny Brown watching over him," Eliza replied as she too relaxed into a canvas deckchair.

"I heard what you said," Lady Penelope said. "You gals think every Saxton daughter should marry a duke. Life doesn't work that way."

Jenny rolled her eyes. "Two of us marry dukes and she thinks it's impossible the third will."

"It's moot anyway," Amelia said. "Warrick intends to obey his father's wishes and marry a woman with a title."

Jenny was reminded of Philip's parents. At one time, they'd adamantly opposed her marriage to their son. She wanted to give her younger sister hope, but she'd had Philip's love to sustain her. It seemed Amelia didn't have that to hold onto. However... "I fought for Philip," she said. "If you want Warrick, you must do the same."

"It would be easier if I knew for sure he cared for me that way," Amelia replied.

~

AMELIA HAD NEVER UNDERSTOOD the appeal of the game of cricket, but it was heartwarming to watch Sax and the lads enjoying themselves—not to mention the antics of the wolfhound. However, her attention inevitably wandered to unusual activity going on in the kitchen garden at the side of the house.

When Wilson appeared with refreshments, she asked him what two men she didn't recognize were doing in the garden.

"Casuals, Miss Saxton," he explained, his nose in the air as he offered the tumblers of lemonade.

"They look rough," Eliza replied, taking a tumbler from the tray.

"Rough doesn't begin to describe them, Your Grace. Judging by the odor, it has been a while since they bathed."

"What on earth are they doing here?" Lady Penelope demanded.

"I would have sent them packing, Ma'am," the butler said. "Mr. Frobisher, the estate manager, hired them as temporary laborers. Mrs. Knight is in a tizzy over it. Our head gardener is none too pleased. Rampling reckons they know nothing about gardening."

"Surely they aren't allowed in the house?" Amelia's mother asked.

"Fortunately for all concerned, Mr. Frobisher has billeted them in the potting shed, well away from the house."

"I suppose there are often transient men looking for work these days," Jenny remarked.

"It has indeed been a lamentable occurrence since the war, Your Grace. Although, I doubt those two were ever in the army. You may be unaware that I myself served. Even a former soldier down on his luck has a certain discipline about him."

"Thank you, Wilson," Amelia said. "I expect you'll keep an eye on them."

"Indeed, Miss Saxton," he assured her as he bowed to the two visiting duchesses and took his leave.

Amelia narrowed her eyes at the men in the garden, shivering when a chill crept across her nape.

CORONATION

Traffic in the streets near Westminster Abbey had ground to a standstill. Warrick, Alex and Philip were obliged to abandon the carriage and make their way on foot through the crowds. Warrick felt uncomfortably conspicuous in his father's ducal robes, but people were respectful and stepped aside.

Dismayed that Philip and Alex had been assigned seats in different parts of the Abbey, Warrick followed the usher to his place in the Lord Steward's box. He didn't know any of the people already seated, but Alex had instructed him to simply use his title as an introduction. His ducal robes would tell the rest, despite the fact they were slightly too small.

"Beaufort," he stated as he sat.

"Gloucester," one fellow responded.

"Norfolk."

"Wessex."

He acknowledged each fellow duke with a nod. Philip had pointed out that he might eventually take part in debates with other peers in the House of Lords, so it was best to make a good impression.

Feeling like a fraud, he decided the best way to do that was to keep his mouth shut.

"I can't wait to see cousin George's much-touted coronation robes," Gloucester declared.

"He's determined to outdo Napoleon," Wessex added. "Even sent a tailor to Paris to study the Little Emperor's robe."

Jaw clenched, Warrick nodded. Alex had already told him of the extravagance.

"We should have a reasonably good view from here," Norfolk remarked. "Beaufort? I say, are you the..."

Warrick almost felt sorry for the fool as his fat face reddened. "Aye. I'm the bastard," he said with no small degree of satisfaction.

So much for good impressions.

A murmur of excitement soughed through the abbey when the royal procession entered, having previously wound its way through the crowded, sun-baked streets.

The King's Royal Herbstrewer and six maids led the way, scattering petals on the carpet. A military band followed, accompanied by a choir who repeatedly sang the anthem *O Lord, grant the King a long life*. Drumming and trumpet fanfares came next. Warrick estimated there must be at least seven hundred people in the procession. Finally, perspiration dripping off the end of his nose, the monarch appeared in his magnificent robes. The congregation gasped and gossiped, clearly not caring they were in a church.

After the procession, a noticeable sigh of relief

echoed off the ancient stones when the Archbishop of Canterbury bade everyone sit.

"It's rumored he'll use the text from the last coronation," Wessex murmured. "Except, of course, there'll be no mention of the Queen."

The three dukes tittered. Warrick knew of the strife between the king and his legal wife. He considered it a national tragedy that a royal prince would comport himself like an philandering dockworker.

"Caroline tried to gain entrance, you know," Gloucester said.

"Never," Norfolk retorted.

"I have it on good authority that at six this morning, her carriage arrived at Westminster Hall and was received with applause from a sympathetic section of the crowd."

"She is popular," Wessex remarked. "Lord knows why."

"The Queen approached on the arm of Lord Hood," Gloucester continued. "She was asked for her ticket by the guard. She replied that the Queen needed no ticket, but was firmly turned away. When they tried to enter by a side door, it was slammed in their faces. Their attempt to find another entrance was blocked by a line of armed soldiers. Then they made for the House of Lords, which is connected to the hall, but she was denied entry there too."

"And that was the end of it, I suppose," Norfolk said.

"Not by a long shot. The party arrived at the abbey, and approached the door right here near Poet's Corner. Lord Hood addressed the doorkeeper."

"I heard professional boxers were hired as guards for the event," Wessex interrupted.

Warrick eyed the burly guard at the nearest doorway and decided Wessex might be right.

"Anyway, Hood said, 'I present to you your Queen, do you refuse her admission?' The doorkeeper replied that he could admit no one without a ticket. After further apparently fruitless argument, the Queen's party retreated, the crowds shouting *Shame! Shame!* as she left in her carriage."

To Warrick this sounded all too much like the kind of conjugal spat he'd heard of in the slums—and did his three fellow dukes have nothing better to natter about on this important occasion? All this drama had apparently taken place just a short while ago, yet the lurid details had already been bandied about.

Once it finally began, the elaborate ceremony dragged on; Warrick had difficulty keeping his eyes open.

Wessex's elbow in his ribs jolted him awake. "Looks like they've misplaced the manuscript text of the coronation oath."

There was an audible collective intake of breath as a flurry of activity erupted around the Coronation chair. Then, a buzzing of relief when George simply signed one of the cards printed with the order of service.

The Archbishop of York preached a lengthy sermon. Warrick had his own ideas about what the prelate's topic should have been. Just a fraction of the expense of this obscenely extravagant affair could have been used to rescue many destitute children from grinding poverty.

Encumbered by the weight of his lavish robes, the obese King perspired heavily throughout the ceremony.

All in all, Warrick found the entire experience sickening.

His dismay grew when he followed the crowd to Westminster Hall where the banquet would be held. Wondering about facilities for the relief of bodily needs, he discovered aristocratic males weren't so different after all. Musing on how the female guests were managing, he joined the group pissing against the ancient walls of Parliament Square.

After much searching, he was glad to discover Alex and Philip had saved him a seat in the hall. He sat with his friends, and waited.

A trumpet fanfare eventually heralded the King's arrival in procession. Things went comically awry when a group of men tried to carry a canopy over the monarch.

"They're the Barons of the Cinque Ports," Alex explained. "It's their traditional right to carry a canopy over the King."

Perhaps wanting to be seen by the crowds, George decided to walk in front of the canopy.

Warrick joined in the sniggering laughter when the elderly barons tried to walk faster. The king eyed the swaying canopy and quickened his pace.

"It's like a comic opera," Philip remarked with disgust.

Already feeling like a caged animal after sitting for hours, Warrick assumed the banquet would now get underway, but the King retired, apparently to rest.

By the time he reappeared in the stiflingly hot hall,

the three ducal friends were among the hundreds of guests continually pelted by large globules of melted wax from more than two thousand candles in the high chandeliers.

Instead of masking the odor of sweat, a myriad of heavy scents only worsened the cloying stink. Ladies swooned. Others fanned themselves with increasing desperation. Earls called for smelling salts for their stricken countesses. Warrick feared he might never breathe fresh air again.

"Thank God our wives didn't attend," Alex said.

"Amen to that," Philip replied.

The noise intensified to full-blown pandemonium when three men rode huge horses into the center of the hall.

"The Deputy Earl Marshal, the Lord High Steward and Lord High Constable," Philip explained, shouting close to Warrick's ear.

Hundreds of servers swarmed out of kitchens adjacent to the hall carrying tureens of soup. From atop their steeds, the three riders patrolled the aisles, overseeing the proceedings.

"This will be interesting," Alex said as the Lord High Steward rode up to the royal head table. "Henry Paget is supposed to dismount and uncover the king's first dish. But he lost a leg at Waterloo. He wears a prothesis designed for riding. Might make things tricky."

Warrick had assumed things couldn't get more ridiculous. However, it became obvious the gentleman was having considerable difficulty dismounting. Amid unbridled laughter from the thousands of guests, he eventually managed with the aid of several pages.

The food set before Warrick was probably delicious but he had lost his appetite. Alex and Philip picked at their portions.

"Is it possible to slip out?" Warrick asked.

"Not unnoticed," Alex replied after looking around. "Besides, the highlight of the banquet is yet to come."

Warrick groaned, feeling overheated in his ducal robes.

Cheers resounded when a man in a full suit of armor rode in through the archway. He galloped the length of the hall, throwing down a gauntlet three times in the traditional challenge.

"The King's Champion," Philip explained. "It's a hereditary title held by the Dymoke family since the 14th century."

"I heard the current holder of the post is a clergyman," Alex said. "So the honor passed to his son. This chap is only twenty years old and does not possess a suitable horse, so the one he's riding was hired from Astley's Circus."

"How appropriate," Philip replied.

Warrick might have laughed if he'd had the energy.

By the time the King processed out after eight o'clock at night, Warrick's body and mind had ceased to function. As they tried to make their way out of the hall, he and his friends sidestepped peers of the realm passed out on the floor. Spectators from the galleries swarmed down to clear the tables of anything they could lay their hands on—food, cutlery, glass, table ornaments, even the gold coronation plates.

Warrick found their scrabbling desperation ironic. Had life turned out differently, he might have been among those filching the mementoes.

Armed soldiers arrived to prevent the looting. Fisticuffs broke out.

"Let's hope George reigns for many years," Alex said when they reached the street. "I couldn't possibly endure this again."

Warrick agreed, but the experience strengthened his resolve to use his newfound title to put an end to the aristocratic excesses he'd witnessed.

A king should look to the welfare of his people.

Volcano

Amelia had fond memories of her indulgent father entertaining his daughters with the creation of a papier-mâché volcano.

Her sisters enthusiastically agreed it would be just the thing to hold the interest of the orphans from Hull and delight Amelia's nephews.

Wilson was eventually coaxed into revealing the location of a teetering pile of old copies of *The Times*, but was horrified by the notion they be torn into strips.

"The old duke has passed away," Amelia pointed out. "What harm in using them for a scientific experiment?"

"The duke's heir may want to read them," he replied.

"Don't you think he'll be more inclined to read current news?" she asked, careful not to reveal Warrick's difficulty with reading.

He eventually capitulated and allowed the lads to carry the newspapers into the schoolroom.

Before they began the experiment, she explained the necessity to build a frame for the volcano. The discussion of possibilities eventually led to the conclusion that some kind of thin wire would be the best idea since it could be bent into shape.

Having volunteered to ask the head gardener if he had any to spare, Tim and Tom rushed off in high spirits.

The schoolroom had a limited supply of Sheffield scissors, and Amelia wasn't yet comfortable putting sharp objects in the lads' hands. In the event, even Avery and Rowland set about gleefully tearing the newspapers into strips. The resulting enormous mound also produced black hands and grinning ink-smeared faces.

While everyone was cleaning up, Tim and Tom returned with a good supply of wire, but Amelia sensed something was wrong. They looked nervous and afraid but, when questioned, averted their eyes and refused to explain. She'd have to speak to Rampling about frightening them.

～

"Here's the only good thing about being in London," Alex said, brandishing a newspaper as he joined Warrick, Philip and other guests for a late breakfast the day after the coronation.

"*The Times* hot off the press," Philip replied with a grin.

Warrick had watched his father devour the news in this same publication and knew of its importance to educated readers. Fortunately, his late father had derived great pleasure from reading pertinent articles aloud, apparently never suspecting his bastard son couldn't read.

When Amelia mentioned needing a goodly amount of newspaper for an experiment she wanted to conduct with the lads, he'd told her about his father's stash of old copies of *The Times*. Making a volcano sounded intriguing, but he suspected Wilson would be protective of the trove.

Warrick's reading skills had improved, but a whole newspaper would be beyond him. Philip knew of his illiteracy. He was relieved when Alex exclaimed, "Listen to this. In London, a mob supporting Queen Caroline rampaged through the West End breaking windows. The Household Cavalry was called in to disperse the rioters."

"Wessex claimed she was popular," Warrick said.

"Elsewhere," Alex continued, "a good-natured crowd watched the ascent of a gas balloon from Green Park and then proceeded to Hyde Park where there was a boat race. In the evening, the trees and The Serpentine were illuminated with lanterns and there was a firework display. All the theaters of London were open free of charge at the King's expense."

"So," Philip said. "The festivities continue. Tonight, we have invitations to several balls. Apparently, the king isn't hosting a celebration at Carlton House. He plans to progress from one ball to the next at some time during the evening."

"Whichever you pick, you'll have to make my excuses," Alex replied. "The hour we spent looking for our carriage last evening depleted what little energy I had left. I plan to get to bed early."

Warrick wasn't surprised. He hadn't suffered catastrophic injuries like those that had befallen Alex at Waterloo. Yet, he too had been exhausted and irritable by the time they fought their way through boisterous crowds and boarded the carriage. They'd dodged several loud arguments between angry noblemen who couldn't find their vehicles among the hundreds clogging the streets.

"Can you give me some hints about the eligible ladies who might be in attendance?" Warrick asked reluctantly. "I'm anxious to do things right."

"Yes, it wouldn't do to pursue married ladies," Philip quipped. "Although I can think of some who'd be only too glad to attract your attention."

"In fact," Alex added. "Philip and I can name at least two duchesses who'll set their caps at you."

"That's alarming," Warrick replied. "Who are these women?"

"You'll know soon enough," Philip replied. "You'll also easily recognize the unattached misses. They'll be looking at you with hope in their eyes and a dance card dangling from their wrists."

"What about titles?"

"Don't worry about that. No matter which event we choose, everybody in attendance will be titled."

Warrick's main preoccupation was suppressing the nervousness that might result in writing his name incorrectly on the dance cards.

He welcomed Philip's suggestion they spend the day touring the city and leave Alex to enjoy his newspaper in peace.

It wasn't easy to persuade the cook to surrender flour for Amelia's experiment. In the end, the lads' wide-eyed pleading convinced her to grudgingly hand it over, along with vinegar and bicarb. Back in the schoolroom, the boys took turns mixing the flour and water to make a paste. They made a mess of themselves and their clothing, but Amelia assured them that was part of the fun. They were all vastly amused—except Tom and Tim who remained subdued. She noticed they kept glancing warily at Kenny and wondered if he'd bullied them. However, what that had to do with the mission to borrow thin wire from the head gardener...

A memory surfaced. Had the boys encountered the two rough men she'd seen the previous day? She resolved to get to the bottom of the problem—but completing the experiment took precedence.

None of her pupils had ever seen a picture of a volcano. Once she drew the basic cone shape on the slate, Charlie and Kenny, as the two eldest, did a fine job of shaping the wire.

Then began the messy task of dipping the newspaper strips in the paste and laying them on the frame. The orphans patiently helped Sax and the two little ones apply the strips. They laughed at Brutus' insistence on licking the volcano. Harmony reigned as they fell into a routine of taking turns.

"They're certainly behaving more like gentlemen," Jenny whispered close to Amelia's ear.

Gratified, she nodded her agreement.

Moans and groans greeted the news that they'd have to leave the volcano to dry overnight. Along with illustrations on the slate, Amelia's explanation of volcanic eruptions and the spectacle they'd see the next day placated them.

Her sisters took their sons to clean up. Heedless of sticky fingers and globs of paste in their hair, the lads hurried out to the forecourt to play a game of cricket before dinner.

Novelty

Philip recommended he and Warrick tour the city on horseback since Alex's driver wasn't familiar with London. Their host gladly loaned them two malleable geldings that he insisted were accustomed to the busy streets.

It soon became obvious to Warrick that his companion knew how to get about in the metropolis. He was aware Philip had been an agent for Whitehall before inheriting the dukedom of Wentworth, but perhaps it was better not to bring that up.

"Over the years, the king has spent untold amounts of money on his residence," Philip explained as they surveyed the dozen or so pillars fronting Carlton House. "Now, he complains it isn't big enough and is spending even more money on refurbishing Buckingham Palace."

"I heard about his pavilion in Brighton," Warrick said.

"I've never seen it," Philip replied. "Apparently, the

onion domes and minarets make it look like something one might see in India or Turkey."

Philip often expressed a desire to change the attitudes of the aristocracy, so Warrick decided it was safe enough to bring up popular discontent with the monarch's lavish lifestyle. "Sooner or later, ordinary people will grow more and more vocal in their opposition to aristocratic privilege."

"You're right, and you've seen it first hand," Philip replied.

"You saw it too when you infiltrated the Hull Corresponding Society."

Philip shook his head. "If only George and his ilk had learned from the assassination attempt. He behaves as if the French Revolution never happened. You and I simply have to keep on pushing for reform."

"I admit I'm nervous about occupying the Beaufort seat in the Lords."

"There's no doubt you'll face censure, opposition, and even ridicule, but I'm sure it won't be the first time in your life you've dealt with opinionated bullies."

Philip's words reassured Warrick to a degree. "I suppose," he allowed.

They rode through Hyde Park, already clogged with carriages. The main thoroughfares teemed with people, all in a hurry to go somewhere, it seemed. Red, white and blue coronation bunting fluttered in the summer breeze. Warrick should have felt at home in a big city, but he realized he'd come to love living in rural Derbyshire, and Amelia was a large part of the reason.

He wished he was back in Cavendish Manor helping to make a volcano.

∽

THE SAXTON SISTERS shared a discreet smile as they ate breakfast the day after construction of the volcano. It was clear the boys couldn't wait to be excused from the table. Even Tim and Tom seemed less subdued.

Her charges scarpered as soon as Amelia said she would meet them in the schoolroom.

Eager faces awaited her when she arrived ten minutes later. Eliza and Jenny accompanied her and brought their sons.

"Who would like to test the volcano to see if the papier-mâché is dry?" she asked.

Every hand shot up, including Sax's.

She tapped her chin and surveyed the group. "Let's see," she said.

"I think Lord Saxton should do it," Kenny offered.

No one had mentioned that Saxton Harcourt was indeed a little boy with a title by virtue of his birth. Somehow, the orphans had picked up on the fact, but Amelia sensed no resentment.

"I'd like to, Aunty Amelia," Sax replied. "But I think the eldest should do it."

His selfless, diplomatic response caused his mother, Eliza, to beam with pride.

Amelia hoped her nephew hadn't felt intimidated by Kenny. The Watkins lad always made it clear he was the head of the gang and the rest often deferred to him. "Very well. Give it a poke and see what you think, Kenny."

Making an obvious effort to hide his nervousness, the boy tapped the side of the structure. "Solid as a rock, Miss Saxton," he declared.

"Time for the fireworks," she replied.

∽

Despite protests that they could each assist the other to dress for the evening's ball, valets were provided for Warrick and Philip by their host. Both were former army batmen. Warrick thought Carlos was fastidious but the former soldier proved to be even more picky about the proper tying of a cravat and the degree of shine on polished boots. Warrick drew the line when the valet insisted his hair be cut shorter in order to be more *the thing*. He eventually agreed to having it tied back in a queue.

"Bloody hell," he exclaimed quietly to Philip when they were both declared suitably attired.

"Indeed," his friend replied with a wry smile, apparently not shocked by the swearing. "But you do want to look your best."

"I feel like a pirate."

"You do look a bit like a swarthy buccaneer," Philip replied. "Women love a rogue."

Warrick didn't consider himself a rogue—rough around the edges, certainly. Once he married, he intended to be a faithful husband, though he was aware most noblemen kept a mistress. He was the result of such a relationship and would never risk bringing bastards into the world. Besides, it was nigh on impossible for a man who lived in the slums to marry happily. Warrick had been given an opportunity to find the right woman; once he did, he would treasure her.

Alex had no objection to letting them take his carriage to the Bradshaw ball, chosen because it was to be held close to their accommodation. Philip also thought there would be fewer pompous aristocrats in attendance. They considered the Duchess of Bradshaw *beyond the pale* thanks to her efforts to promote education for women.

"Sounds like two duchesses I know," Warrick quipped, though his thoughts went to Amelia. If her enlightened father hadn't seen to her education, Warrick would be the loser. He owed her so much more than he could ever repay.

That truth dogged him as he ascended the long, winding staircase to the upper floor of the Duke of Bradshaw's London townhouse. Philip introduced him to their host and hostess. "Welcome, Your Grace," the elderly duchess said, extending her hand. "I've been anxious to meet you."

"Thank you for the invitation, Your Grace," he replied, brushing a kiss on her knuckles. "Your home is charming."

"Be prepared to be the curiosity of the day," Philip warned after they'd shaken the duke's hand and entered the ballroom.

"The bastard duke, you mean," Warrick replied.

"The Regent who's finally become King is old news. You're a novelty," Philip declared, slapping him on the back. "Now, go forth and find a bride."

ERUPTION

Nobody breathed when Charlie poured the vinegar into the opening at the top of the volcano. Amelia had explained about volcanic eruptions, but hadn't told her pupils exactly what would happen when the vinegar came into contact with the bicarbonate of soda carefully spooned in beforehand by Eddie.

Squeals of delight filled the schoolroom when the foamy *lava* flowed over the sides of the volcano. Brutus growled, obviously not knowing what to make of the event. The sight of the tough-as-nails lads transformed into wide-eyed little boys brought tears to Amelia's eyes. She'd come to love these orphans.

The prospect of leaving them and Cavendish Manor couldn't be borne, but her departure would be inevitable when Warrick found his heiress.

"Again, please, Aunty Amelia," Sax pleaded, sweeping away her melancholy.

Brutus echoed his request with a loud bark.

By the time everyone took a turn pouring in the vinegar or spooning the bicarb, the top of the volcano was soggy.

"Our cone looks rather sad," Amelia said. "We'll let it dry then see what needs to be repaired tomorrow."

"Aw," came the chorus of disappointment.

"Lunch now, then a quick game of cricket before lessons resume at two o'clock."

"You're so good with them," Eliza said, picking up Avery as the boys trooped out. "That brilliant demonstration brought back fond memories of Papa."

Propped on his mother's hip, Amelia's nephew held out his arms to her and flexed his pudgy fingers.

"You've even charmed this little one," her sister jested as she handed over the toddler.

"You always insisted it was your destiny to be an educator," Jenny said. "And you were right."

Amelia nuzzled Avery's blond hair, saddened that it seemed her destiny didn't include a family of her own. "Ready for some lunch, young man?" she asked with a sigh.

He cupped her face and kissed her cheek in reply.

∽

WARRICK FILLED his lungs to settle his nerves. Gloved hands clasped behind his back, he strode across the ballroom floor and approached a young woman named Lady Felicia Montague. Tall, willowy and blond, she was the youngest daughter of the Earl of Hansbury. According to Philip, she was considered the season's catch, thanks in no small part to a substantial dowry. Warrick wasn't interested in the dowry, but Lady Felicia had an attractive smile and the body to go with it. "Beaufort," he announced, feeling like a stuffed shirt as he bent at the waist.

"Lady Felicia Montague," she replied, offering her gloved hand.

He performed the necessary polite ritual, assuming nervousness was contributing to his cock's lack of interest. Or perhaps it was her cloying perfume.

"I'd be honored if you'd allow me to sign your dance card," he said, parroting Philip perfectly.

"I'm given to understand your seat is in Derbyshire," she replied, her nasally voice making *Derbyshire* sound like the depths of hell.

Tempting though it was to point out he was actually born and bred in Hull's dockland, he clenched his jaw and nodded.

She looked him up and down as if he were a horse on the auction block. "You are easy on the eye," she finally purred. "However, I have my heart set on marrying someone from the southern counties."

"Of course," he said as he bowed politely and walked away to rejoin his friend at the refreshment table.

"I wouldn't marry that bitch if she were the last woman on earth," he growled.

"Did I not mention her reputation for bitchiness?" Philip replied, sipping his ratafia. "Sorry. Must have slipped my mind."

It appeared Philip wasn't inclined to take the matter of finding a bride seriously, but Warrick pressed on. He had more luck with his next attempt. Lady Timothea St. Andrews agreed to partner him in the quadrille. In the course of the figures, her copious breasts came close to bouncing right out of her low cut gown, but he found the experience comical rather than arousing. He wasn't the only man who missed a step or two. It was difficult to concentrate on the dance when tits might overflow and nipples put in an appearance. Nevertheless, he offered to escort this daughter of a marquess to the refreshment table where they procured glasses of lemonade.

"So, you're the illegitimate fellow," she said, preempting his efforts to think of a way to begin the conversation.

"I am," he replied, the lemonade suddenly leaving a sour taste.

"How interesting," she said. "Not that I mind. In fact..."

She prattled on and on about bastardy and illegitimacy and the dreadful state of public morals, the blame for which lay squarely at the door of the common man. Warrick wondered if a good slap might knock her off her high horse. Instead, he excused himself and went in search of Philip. "Any other brilliant suggestions?" he asked sarcastically.

His next three partners were pleasant women—attractive, good conversationalists—but he simply didn't see himself spending the rest of his life with any one of them. They didn't trigger any emotional or physical response.

"Let's face it," Philip said when a dejected Warrick found him again. "None of the women here tonight are going to measure up to Amelia in your estimation. Or in mine, for that matter."

So, that was Philip's ploy!

"But..."

"I know. Your father wanted you to marry a noblewoman. However, I believe he'd also want you to be happy. Amelia makes you happy."

"Is it that obvious?"

"When a man's smitten with a woman, it's almost impossible for him to hide his feelings."

"She might not feel the same."

"That's rubbish, and you know it."

The tight knot in Warrick's gut loosened. He was about to suggest they leave when rumor of the king's arrival spread through the assembly.

The urge to return to Cavendish Manor seethed inside him, but they couldn't leave until the preening monarch moved on to the next ball.

∼

ANXIOUS TO GET on with the lesson she'd prepared for the afternoon, Amelia printed the word POMPEII on the slate. It wasn't unusual for the lads to lose track of time when they were playing cricket, but they were already fifteen minutes late.

She startled when Eddie and Charlie burst into the schoolroom, both yelling. She balked when Eddie grasped her arm. "I can't understand a word you're saying," she chided. "Calm down and tell me what's wrong."

Eddie swallowed hard. "Kenny's pa," he panted breathlessly. "In the garden."

Fear tightened Amelia's throat. Her heart raced as guilt surged. She made the connection right away. Why hadn't she paid attention to the feelings of dread prompted by the new casual laborers?

Her trembling knees threatened to buckle when Charlie shouted, "He's killed the dog and taken Lord Saxton, too."

Outrage trounced fear. She flew out of the schoolroom like an avenging angel, the two lads hard on her heels.

"The Spaniard tried to stop them," Eddie said. "But they beat him."

She emerged from the house in time to see the thugs disappear into a grove of trees, Sax and Kenny slung over their shoulders like sacks of grain. Brutus lay motionless. Aided by Tim and Tom, Carlos struggled to his feet in the forecourt.

"Said 'e'd kill us if we told, Miss," Tim wailed, his face wet with tears.

Again, Amelia had failed to pay attention to intuition. Lifting her skirts, she hurried in pursuit of the kidnappers. "Stop," she yelled breathlessly when she caught sight of them five minutes later. She questioned the wisdom of her actions when the bigger of the two men stopped abruptly and turned to snarl at her.

"Do you realize you're kidnapping the son of a duke?" she shouted, gripping the trunk of a tree like a shipwreck survivor clinging to flotsam. "It's a hanging offense."

He threw his son to the ground. Kenny edged away

from his father, until the brute ordered him to be still. He obeyed, terror in his eyes.

"If it ain't Farrell's fancy piece," Watkins growled as he stalked toward her.

"I am no such thing," she retorted, alarmed by the smirk on his dirty face.

"The lads say diff'rent," he said. "I owe Farrell but we canna 'ang about fer 'im any longer. See 'ow 'e feels when I take summat from 'im."

Almost before she realized what was happening, she'd been hoisted over his shoulder.

The brute kicked Kenny hard and ordered him to get on his feet. "Follow yon Freddie," he spat.

Scarcely able to breathe for the stench of male sweat and the boney shoulder digging into her belly as he loped off, she urged Kenny to run, but no sound emerged from her constricted throat.

The sobbing lad stumbled to keep ahead of his father.

She pummeled Watkins' back with her fists, but he paid no mind as he carried her deeper into the woods.

MISCHIEF

Neither Philip nor Alex wanted to stay in London a moment longer. Warrick was relieved, but would have found some means of traveling north on his own if needs be. He'd faced the truth—that Amelia was the wife he wanted and needed — but he dreaded his proposal would come too late. He couldn't rid himself of the premonition she'd left Cavendish Manor in his absence.

Though the three dukes departed before dawn, it took until dusk to reach Northampton. The sun-baked, rutted roads were clogged with horses, coaches, carts and wagons. It seemed the nobility weren't the only ones who had ventured south for the coronation. Warrick found himself biting his nails, a habit he'd cured himself of years ago.

They stayed overnight at the same inn, ate in the same private dining room, but Warrick acknowledged he wasn't the same man who'd made the journey to London. Philip and Alex had insisted all along that he'd been given the opportunity to make a difference, to crack the aristocratic mold. Yet, he'd been determined to enter into the kind of loveless aristocratic marriage his father deemed wise. But his father belonged to a different generation and Warrick lived in changing times. The realization was freeing but, at the same time terrifying. What if Amelia rejected him? He was the Duke of Beaufort but, inside, he'd always be plain old Warrick Farrell.

"You're very quiet tonight," Philip observed as they dined on Melton Mowbray pork pies and mash.

"Just anxious to get to Cavendish," he replied.

"As am I," Alex agreed. "I have this strange feeling something has gone awry."

Philip nodded. "I admit to having the same feeling of unease. Maybe we are just missing our families."

"Nevertheless," Warrick replied. "I suggest we leave at first light."

The humid heat and dreams of lying naked with Amelia made for a restless night and an uncomfortable morning erection.

~

THE CALL of a screech owl woke Amelia from her doze. The weedy ground beneath her was damp, the tree at her back unyielding. Night crawlers, and worse, likely abounded in these woods. It didn't bear thinking about. She tightened her arms around Sax who stirred in his sleep. He'd hadn't cried during the hours-long trek through forest, meadow and bog. He must have seen Brutus struck down, but hadn't said a word about his loyal puppy's demise. "Brave little man," she whispered, peering across the glade at Kenny. She could barely see his huddled form in the darkness, but sensed he was awake and likely freezing. Lying between them, hogging the warmth of the fire's embers and the only blanket, his father snored loudly. The wretch he called *The Ferret* was supposedly keeping watch somewhere out of sight.

The summer sun had beaten down on them mercilessly when they'd traversed open ground. Kenny had doffed his cap and given it to Sax. It was much too large for the child, but she was grateful for Kenny's thoughtful sacrifice. For the first time in her life, she wished she owned one of the ubiquitous caps. The rare copse offered welcome shade but her nose must be burned beet red.

The day was sweltering, but they weren't dressed for the cool night. Encased in muddy, wet boots, her toes soon froze. As darkness fell, she'd beckoned Kenny to cuddle with her and Sax but his father had kicked him away. No son of his was going to grow up a sissy.

The situation was desperate, but she hoped her presence was of some comfort to the two boys. Any sign of Kenny's swagger had disappeared. Fear of his brutish father had rendered him mute.

They'd had nothing to eat or drink since the kidnapping, but neither had their captors. Sooner or later, Watkins would have to venture closer to a village or hamlet; she doubted if either of the city dwellers knew how to trap rabbits or other small game.

The boys had managed to relieve their bladders during the day. She'd had no such opportunity and would rather soil herself than ask these ruffians for any favors.

She held on to the hope they would be tracked. Alex would move heaven and earth to rescue his beloved son and heir, although she doubted Warrick and his friends had even left the coronation festivities that were touted to go on for days.

She grieved for her sister. Eliza must be going out of her mind with worry for her little boy. Surely the local magistrate in Derby would have been summoned and a search party organized.

She wasn't familiar with the landscape of Derbyshire but thought they were headed into the Peak District. That possibility gave her hope. The rougher terrain would slow down their progress.

She and Warrick had planned to trek the hills and dales with his wards. If only she'd confessed her feelings for him, he might have changed his determination to marry a titled heiress. Now, it was too late.

She leaned her head back against the tree and let the tears flow.

∼

RELIEF FLOODED Warrick when Cavendish Manor finally came into view, but his optimism was short-lived. It was nearly dusk, yet the forecourt of his home was clogged with vehicles of all shapes and sizes. Men he didn't recognize hurried about. Light blazed in every window.

"Something's wrong," Philip declared, echoing Warrick's fears.

Despite his limp, Alex bounded from the carriage when Eliza emerged from the house and ran toward them. He caught his distraught wife when she collapsed into his arms, blubbering incoherently.

"Tell me slowly what's happened," Alex said.

"Sax has been kidnapped," she wailed.

Philip moved to support his lifelong friend when he swayed alarmingly.

Warrick had only to look at the stricken faces of his wards gathered around the front door to know that wasn't the extent of the mischief that had gone on. Jenny was waddling hurriedly to Philip. But where was Amelia?

"Who has taken him?" Alex asked, his voice dripping ice.

"Kenny Watkins' father," Jenny exclaimed.

Warrick clenched his fists. "I should have killed the wretch when I had the chance," he growled.

Suddenly, Tim was on his knees, looking up at Warrick. "I'm so sorry," he cried. "'E came for Kenny, but threatened to kill me and Tom if we told."

Warrick cursed his own stupidity. He'd naively thought he could protect his lads simply by bringing them to Derbyshire. Instead, evil had followed them.

"How long have they been gone?" Philip asked.

"Since yesterday afternoon," Jenny replied. "They beat Carlos senseless when he tried to stop them. The magistrate has organized the locals into a search party, but there's been no sign of them so far. They've called off the search for the night."

"Brutus will be able to track Sax," Alex declared resolutely. "Even in the dark."

Eliza's wail grew louder.

"Brutus lies at death's door," Jenny explained hoarsely, her cheeks wet with tears. "They slashed him with a knife when he tried to protect Sax."

Grieving for Alex's torment, Warrick scanned the forecourt, desperate to delay asking the question that gnawed at him.

Jenny put an arm on his sleeve. "They took Amelia as well."

Warrick seethed. The treasured jewel he should have protected was in the hands of a ruthless thug. "I'd lay odds on the identity of his partner in crime," he hissed.

"Freddie the Ferret," Charlie confirmed as he joined them.

PIGEON PIE

Amelia was counting on hunger clouding Watkins' thoughts and driving him to make mistakes. His girth suggested a man not used to controlling his appetite. "These boys need to eat something for breakfast if we are to continue this madness," she insisted, earning the threat of a backhander from the snarling Watkins. She was spared the violence when Kenny dove in front of her and was felled by the blow.

"Brute," she shouted, helping the lad to rise. "Is it any wonder your son ran away."

"Thank you," she whispered to Kenny before his cursing father seized him.

Sax took hold of her hand. She was angry her young nephew had witnessed the violence, but he'd also seen Kenny's selfless action. Squeezing his hand, she prayed her presence was of some reassurance.

In the daylight, she could see that the higher ground of the Peak District was yet a long way off. Disappointment and relief warred within her. She didn't have the stamina to tackle the climb, but had hoped slower progress would increase the chances of rescue.

She wondered if Freddie Ferret had abandoned his partner, but he soon entered the clearing with arms full of kindling.

"Me stomach thinks me throat's cut," he complained, dropping his bundle of twigs.

Watkins shoved his son toward the blackened remains of the fire. "Meck thasel' useful," he growled.

Kenny managed to coax a meager flame from the embers and the fire crackled to life after emitting clouds of choking smoke. The warmth chased away some of the morning's damp. Amelia saw no other purpose since they'd nothing to cook on the fire.

"Didst see a cottage or owt?" Watkins asked his ferret.

"Aye. A few, in yon vale."

"Then why didn't tha filch summat t'eat?"

Freddie scratched his head. "Aye. Couldav."

It took him a moment to realize Watkins was glaring at him. He finally got the message and scurried off.

Sax cuddled into Amelia when she sat as close to the fire as she could. "Papa always tells me never to give up hope," he whispered. "Things are never as bad as they seem."

"He would be so proud of his brave son," she replied, choking back tears.

"I try to be like Papa," he said.

Amelia swallowed the lump in her throat. Young as

he was, Sax was aware of the painful physical challenges his father had overcome.

∼

"I'm not a veterinarian, but I think he'll be fine in a week," Philip said as he stroked the groaning dog's head.

Warrick knew Philip had done his best for the wolfhound. That the animal had survived at all was testament to his skills. The bandage around his belly covered an impressive row of neat stitches.

The three dukes had led search parties. They'd ridden from dawn to dusk in the direction they assumed Watkins had gone to get back to Hull. Believing the kidnappers would avoid populated areas, they traversed marshlands, meadows and forests.

But they needed the dog's tracking skills.

"Grateful as I am," Alex growled. "A week's too long. My wife is at her wits' end."

Warrick was concerned for his friend. Alex had aged years in just two days. His limp had worsened considerably.

Warrick kept his own frantic despair to himself. Everyone was upset enough about Amelia's disappearance without him drawing attention to his own loss.

Guilt consumed him. He should have foreseen Watkins' determination to retrieve his son and exact revenge. He'd left Cavendish Manor completely unprotected—and for what? The coronation had been a farce, the hunt for a *suitable* wife a fiasco.

At least he'd finally come to his senses as far as Amelia was concerned, but it might be too late.

~

Freddie returned to the camp, a triumphant grin on his weaselly face, crumbs dotting his scraggly beard. "Ta da," he declared, holding aloft a pie with the outer ring of the crust nibbled off.

Watkins leapt to his feet and grabbed the remains of the pie.

"Pidgin," Freddie said as Watkins bit into the pastry. "Yon goodwife left it on t' winderledge."

"Are you going to scoff the lot?" Amelia demanded.

"What's it to thee?" the ruffian replied, his mouth full.

She'd already seen where his temper might lead, but somebody had to stand up to the bully. "If you expect these boys to walk all the way to Hull without sustenance, you're more brainless than I thought."

"Mebbe I'll get rid of yon lordling," he threatened, waving a hand at Sax. "One less mouth to feed. Thee an' all. Interfering wench."

"Nay," Freddie said, licking his lips as he eyed the disappearing pie. "I'll nay be party to murder."

Grumbling, Watkins threw what remained of the pie at Amelia's feet. "Goin' fer a piss," he told the Ferret as he trudged off into the trees. "Keep an eye."

Thankful to be spared the sight of him relieving himself, Amelia salvaged what was left of the food from the smashed dish—probably a prized possession of some farmer's wife. She divided it in two and gave the portions to Kenny and Sax.

"Take part of mine," Kenny said, breaking off a chunk for her.

"And mine, Aunty," Sax said.

Reluctant as she was to take food from them, it was important to keep up her strength if she was to watch for any opportunity to escape.

"Wish I could be as brave as you, Miss Saxton," Kenny said.

"I'm not brave," she replied. "I'm just determined not to let them see my fear."

BULLY

"We could wander aimlessly all over Derbyshire and never find them," Philip opined on the third day as they prepared to join another search. "We know where they are headed. Better to be waiting on the outskirts of Hull for them to arrive."

Alex shook his head, his face haggard. "They might not survive that long."

Alex was perhaps correct but Warrick conceded Philip had the right idea. "Amelia's strong. She'll keep the boys alive."

"I don't think Eliza will cope if anything happens to our son," Alex said.

Warrick would be devastated if Amelia were lost to him, but Alex was clearly exhausted. "I suggest Philip and I ride to Yorkshire."

Alex struggled to stand. "I'll come with you."

Philip put a hand on his friend's arm. "You're in no fit state to ride so far. Besides, Eliza needs you here."

"What about Brutus?" Alex asked. "He's still our best chance of tracking them."

Indecision played across Philip's face as he gnawed his bottom lip.

Warrick made the decision for him. "We could rig up a sling. Take him with us."

The dog might not survive the trek, but if taking him gave Alex hope...

～

As they trudged wearily across what she thought might be north Lincolnshire, Amelia noticed a change in Kenny. He no longer cowered in fear when his father berated him or threatened a beating. In fact, he sneered at his tormentor.

Watkins was clearly puzzled by this behavior. Amelia recognized his confusion as typical of a bully whose power lay in his victim's fear. Common sense should open his eyes to the fact his son had grown into a sturdy young man. If it came to a physical confrontation, Kenny's youth and agility might prove too much for his father's lumbering girth.

As they drew closer to Yorkshire, the danger increased. Their captor would have no reason to free her and Sax once he had his son hidden away in the slums. She took the change in Kenny as a positive sign. Exhausted, hungry and filthy, she could do little on her own, but with the lad's help...

On the fourth night, Kenny crept over to join her and Sax after his father's snoring began. "I'm not going to let him hurt you and your nephew, Miss Saxton," he whispered.

"We must be very careful," she replied.

"Just have to delay things until Warrick comes to rescue us," he said. "And he will come."

Amelia had tried desperately to hold on to that hope. Kenny's faith in Warrick renewed her own. "I know he will," she replied, drawing the lad closer so they could share warmth.

"Have you noticed Freddie's non-stop whining has also ceased," she said. "I suspect he's worried about Watkins' intentions once we reach our destination. He seems increasingly reluctant to do his partner's bidding."

"No surprise there. Freddie's been treated no differently from us. Pa hogs the blanket, the fire and the food."

"Even though it's the ferret who has stolen what little sustenance we've had and scrounged the wood."

Kenny sat up straight. "I'm sick of being my father's whipping boy. I like my new life with you and Warrick and I intend to fight for it. I'd rather die than go back to hell."

Amelia prayed it wouldn't come to that.

∽

SIX HOURS after leaving Cavendish Manor, the two dukes rode into the courtyard of Philip's home, Wentworth Manor. They'd made good time on the mostly flat terrain of their route, stopping only to ask the occasional field laborers if they'd seen any sign of the motley group. No one had.

Despite his compulsion to ride on, Warrick was forced to agree with his friend that the horses were spent and dusk was creeping across the wold. Wentworth Manor's stables would provide fresh mounts for the morrow.

In the end, they'd decided not to bring Brutus. The likelihood of the dog dying en route and the added strain on the horses tipped the balance in favor of relying on human intuition.

After a most welcome bath, they sat down for dinner and discussed the best plan of action.

"They may have traveled further west of here," Philip said, spreading out a map of the area. "Crossing the Trent and then the Ouse would be much easier than tackling the Humber itself."

Warrick considered what he knew of Watkins. "That would put him a good way west of Hull itself. He's lazy and probably tired of walking."

"If they are still on foot," Philip pointed out.

"A stolen carriage, or horses, would mean traveling by road. He'll want to stick to cross country paths. We have to assume they are on foot, and that Amelia and Sax are with them."

The alternative didn't bear thinking about.

"So, you think he'll try to cross the Humber?"

"Yes. He's done it many times before. Any man born and raised in Hull is familiar with the shifting sands and tides of the river. Particularly if he's engaged in smuggling contraband from Scandinavia and Europe."

Philip scratched his newly-shaven chin. "There used to be a ferry from South Ferriby. I have contacts there but, these days, the paddle steamer goes from New Holland."

Warrick studied the map. "He'll not walk as far as New Holland and wouldn't board a paying ferry in any case, especially with hostages in tow. Stealing a boat is more his style."

"But it's a long way to row, as we both remember."

Warrick chuckled, recalling the ruse they had concocted to convince the villainous Derrick Peploe that he had drowned Philip in the river. "Knowing Watkins, he'll not be doing the rowing."

"Hard work, as I recall," Philip jested, rubbing his bicep as they shared the humor of Warrick obliging his *victim* to row to his own fake death. "I still think it's worth stopping in South Ferriby. Swede Nelthorpe's a good friend and he knows everything that goes on along this side of the river. If he doesn't, he'll have a relative who does."

DROWNED RATS

When Watkins finally called a halt, Amelia collapsed to her knees in the damp grass. She shivered in the stiff breeze rippling the surface of a wide river. She'd never seen the Humber before, but every Yorkshire lass had heard tales of its legendary tides and shifting sands. Her home county was barely visible on the opposite bank but may as well have been a thousand miles away.

Standing close by, Kenny eased Sax to the ground. He'd carried her exhausted nephew on his back for miles. Unaware of the increased danger they were in, Sax curled up in a tight ball.

Watkins and Freddie had walked away into the tall reeds along the bank.

"Surely your father doesn't intend to take us across the river?" she asked Kenny, hating the hoarse despair in her voice. Was it foolish to hope rescue might yet be possible—or was it too late? Why had Warrick not come?

"Of course," the lad replied, pulling her away from

Sax so he wouldn't hear. "Considers himself the king of smugglers."

"But I don't see a ferry, or any means to cross."

"He'll steal a boat. That's what they're searching for now."

Amelia looked out over the dark water. She'd fight tooth and nail if Watkins tried to force her and Sax into a boat. The brute had no intention of taking them to Hull. An *accidental* drowning would suit his purposes.

"This is our last chance," Kenny said, clearly of the same mind. "Pa'll toss thee both o'erboard. Freddie too, I shouldn't wonder."

As if conjured by the mention of his name, the Ferret emerged from the reedy bank, waving his skinny arms. "Come wi' me," he panted. "'Ad to go nigh on all the way to Ferriby to find a boat."

Hope flickered in Amelia's breast. Were they close to a village?

"You know he'll drown everyone except me," Kenny warned.

Doubt flickered briefly in Freddie's eyes, but then he shook his head. "Nay. Come on. Yon fisher didn't take kindly to losin' 'is boat. 'E's likely gone to get 'elp."

"We're not going any further," Amelia declared, hands on hips. Her resolve shattered when Freddie scooped up Sax and loped away.

"Stay here," Kenny shouted as he ran off in pursuit.

It was the safest place for her, but she couldn't abandon her darling nephew.

WARRICK FEARED they were wasting precious time recounting the dire situation to the innkeeper Philip knew in South Ferriby. His fellow duke insisted Swede Nelthorpe was their best chance. "This area is the Nelthorpe family's little kingdom," he explained. "Nothing goes on hereabouts that Swede doesn't know about."

"Iffen 'e's comin' from that direction," Swede said when they'd finished the tale, "Me cuzin Alfred keeps a fishin' boat ont' bank."

Shouting instructions to someone in the kitchen to *keep an eye*, he led them outside and pointed to the west. "'Alf a mile, or so, I reckon."

Warrick and Philip remounted. They hadn't ridden far when they encountered an elderly fellow limping his way to the village.

"Alfred Nelthorpe?" Philip asked.

"Aye, Yer Grace," the man panted, apparently recognizing his local duke.

Close to desperation, Warrick couldn't believed something might finally have gone right. "Someone stole your boat?"

"Aye. A big bugger," Alfred confirmed, studying his feet when he realized he'd used foul language. "Beg pardon, Yer Grace. Yonder, by me wee 'ut."

The two friends galloped as far as a dilapidated lean-to in time to see an overloaded rowboat several yards off shore. "The outgoing tide will take it soon," Philip shouted urgently, pointing to the swiftly moving current in the middle of the river. "Is anybody at the oars?"

"That's not the least of the problems," Warrick

replied, his heart lurching as the boat tipped alarmingly. Amelia, Watkins and Kenny were all on their feet, struggling for control of Sax. "He's trying to throw the boy overboard."

Both men dismounted quickly and waded into the reeds. Tearing off his frock coat, Warrick almost stepped on Freddie's body but didn't stop to see if the wretch were alive. It was doubtful, given the gaping hole at the ferret's throat.

When the water reached his waist, Warrick heard Amelia's shriek. He plunged head first into the fast-flowing waters, Philip not far behind.

～

AMELIA SHRIEKED when she lost her grip on Sax and Watkins threw him into the river. Without hesitation, she jumped in to save her nephew, remembering only as the water closed over her head that she couldn't swim. Her sodden half boots weighed her down. Ruined skirts clung to her legs.

She was sinking...sinking...too tired and heartbroken to care.

Then, suddenly, something or somebody was hauling her up...up, but her lungs might burst before...

She gulped air when she broke the surface. She was alive...but Sax...

"I've got you," a familiar voice said. "Don't fight me. Philip has your nephew."

"You came," she croaked, confident the strong arm clamped around her ribs would see her safely to shore.

"We've been searching for days," he said raggedly, helping her lie down on the bank after dragging her through the reeds.

She rolled onto her side as water surged up her throat. When the retching stopped, the uncontrollable shivering began. Warrick gathered her into his arms and held her tightly.

She'd longed to be held like this, close to his thudding heart, but... "I must look like the wreck of the *Minotaur*," she said, embarrassed for him to see her so filthy and bedraggled. What must he think of her retching in front of him? And the *Minotaur*? Could she sound any more pretentious?

"You are the beautiful, red-nosed woman I love, Amelia Saxton. Will you do me the honor of becoming my wife?"

Startled, she lifted her gaze and looked into the soulful eyes of the man she adored. He'd lost his cravat to the river. The sodden shirt clung to his powerful body. His wet hair was plastered to his head. Her pirate rogue had rescued her and she couldn't stifle the laughter bubbling in her throat. "We look like two drowned rats," she exclaimed, dissolving into a fit of giggles interspersed with hiccups. She eventually managed to choke out a *yes* to his proposal.

The giggles turned to tears when Philip, soaked to the skin, delivered a shivering Sax into her arms. "Precious boy," she murmured into his wet hair.

"I told you they would come," he said with a smug grin.

Having been alerted to the drama by his cousin, Swede Nelthorpe arrived at the river bank with a group of men and quickly took charge. Amelia and Sax were swathed in warm blankets. Warrick mounted his horse and insisted Amelia be lifted into his arms. He had no intention of ever losing sight of her. Philip took Sax up on his horse and cradled the boy on his lap. Freddie's body was retrieved from the reeds and loaded onto a dog cart.

Within ten minutes, everyone was back at the inn. Messengers were dispatched to alert Alex and Eliza that their son was safe.

Two hours later, after they'd bathed, dressed in borrowed clothing and been fed a hearty meal, Amelia tucked Sax into a bed with fresh linens. Watching her, Warrick's heart swelled. His children would be blessed with a wonderful mother. His own mother had loved him in her way, but gin had stolen her motherly instincts.

"I pray this harrowing experience won't haunt the courageous lad," Amelia whispered.

"If he proves to be as resilient as his father, he'll weather the storm," he replied.

Warrick, Philip and Amelia then sat down in a private dining room and began earnest discussions about the harsh reality they hadn't wanted to address. Things had turned out well for all concerned, except Kenny. Watkins had escaped across the Humber and taken his son with him.

"We have to rescue him," Amelia exclaimed, tears

welling. "Sax and I wouldn't have survived without his help."

Warrick knew there was more to it than that. Like him, she'd come to think of the lads as family. He covered Amelia's hand with his own. "Don't you worry. I'll get him back."

Aristocratic Blackmail

"I wish you didn't have to go," Amelia told Warrick the morning after the rescue.

He'd said nothing more about their relationship since the dramatic proposal on the riverbank. Of course, this was their first opportunity to be alone together—and it was beyond inappropriate for her to have come to his room. However, she had to know if his offer of marriage had been prompted by a guilty conscience—or perhaps by overwhelming relief the captives had been found alive.

His own clothes had been thoroughly cleaned and dried. Even his boots were shiny. Carlos would be proud of the intricate arrangement of the borrowed cravat. She briefly wondered who in this rural backwater knew how to accomplish such a thing.

Warrick the pirate rogue had once more become the Duke of Beaufort, a man far above her touch.

"Come, put your finger on this knot," he replied.

It wasn't the response she was expecting but it drew

her attention to the bundle he'd been busily tying up with string.

She put her finger on the half knot.

Heat flooded her when he reached around from behind and tightened the knot on her finger.

"All done," he whispered, his warm breath on her nape stealing her wits.

She expected him to remove his arms from around her waist.

Instead, he turned her to face him and bent his head.

Her spirits soared when he touched his lips to hers. She put her arms around his neck, sifting her fingers through the silky hair at his nape as he deepened the kiss and pulled her closer. His tongue demanded entry and she allowed it willingly. He plundered her mouth greedily, taking no pains to disguise his body's hunger for her. She was an innocent, but her married sisters had hinted at the delights of sexual congress. The carnal power of his assault on her senses ignited a burning desire to join their bodies, to know for herself the joy of intimacy with a man.

Warrick rested his forehead against hers when they broke apart for breath. "We'd better stop, else I take you here and now," he rasped.

This was the Warrick she loved. The man who knew what he wanted and made no bones about it. No flowery aristocratic lovemaking for Warrick Farrell. "I love you," she whispered, unashamedly pressing her mons to his hard maleness.

"I know," he admitted. "And I've loved you from the

moment I first saw you. I let my father's wishes cloud my better judgement. You were made for me."

Her heart rejoiced, but he was leaving. "I just wish this was all over."

"It will be. As soon as we're back in Derbyshire, I'll obtain a special license and we'll wed."

"But first…"

He nodded. "Philip and I will go to Hull and alert the magistrates to Watkins' crimes. The testimony of two dukes should seal his fate—kidnapping of a duke's son and sister-in-law, theft, murder, and attempted murder."

"But…"

He touched a finger to her lips. "He'll have to be caught and apprehended before he can be prosecuted." He picked up the bundle. "That's where these come in. Swede has provided what I need to pass unnoticed through the slums. It's the only way to flush him out."

"I wish I could come with you."

"Absolutely not," he retorted. "Alex and Eliza will no doubt be here later today to reunite with Sax. Go to Beverley with them and wait for Kenny and me to come for you. You need to rest after your ordeal."

A rap at the door heralded Philip's arrival.

"I must go," Warrick said, pecking a kiss on her forehead.

"No, Your Grace," she declared, grasping his arm. "Nice as Beaufort's kisses are, I want a Warrick Farrell kiss."

With a lustful glint in his eyes and a smug smile, he obliged.

After knocking twice more, Philip coughed and announced he'd be waiting downstairs.

"Don't come down," Warrick said when he eventually took his leave.

She held back the tears until the sound of his footsteps on the stairs faded. He refused to expose her to the dangers of the slums, but he'd also be in danger if any of the former members of the Hull Corresponding Society saw through his disguise. In their view, he was a traitor who'd helped thwart their plot to assassinate the Regent at York's racecourse. Worse than that, he'd betrayed his roots by becoming a toff.

~

Warrick and Philip rode to the ferry dock at New Holland where they boarded the paddle steamer. After a choppy, two mile voyage, they disembarked the PS Caledonia in Hull. Philip still owned a townhouse in the city and it was there they spent the night.

The following morning, they met with the Mayor. After driving Warrick mad by scratching every detail in a ledger with a blunt quill, Charles Whitaker recommended they accompany him to visit the High Sheriff.

Visibly shocked by the horror and extent of Watkins' crimes, Mr. Craven nevertheless dithered. "He kidnapped the boy and his aunt in Derbyshire, you say."

"Correct," Warrick said, wondering where this line of questioning was leading.

"But the murder of this ferret person took place in Lincolnshire?"

"I don't see..." Warrick began, getting the feeling Craven was trying to shirk responsibility.

"So he hasn't actually committed crimes in Yorkshire?" the High Sheriff asked, though he already knew the answer. "Perhaps this is a matter for the Derbyshire Assizes?"

Fortunately, Philip stepped in before Warrick succumbed to the temptation to throttle the fellow. "My dear Craven," he said in a haughty, aristocratic voice Warrick had never heard him use before. The only thing missing was the quizzing glass. "Are you truly willing to risk the wrath of three dukes and the outrage of the populace by passing this matter on to a different jurisdiction? My ducal seat is in Lincolnshire, as you are aware, but I am well known in Hull."

"But, Your Grace," Craven began.

Philip waved off the interruption like a pesky fly. "Last time I checked," he continued, "Derbyshire and Lincolnshire were still part of this United Kingdom. Kidnapping and murder are offenses against the Crown, are they not?"

It was the kind of aristocratic blackmail Warrick abhorred in normal circumstances, but the Mayor nodded.

"You're right, Your Grace," Whitaker admitted. "However, we can't send watchmen to scour the slums for this Watkins fellow. They might not make it out alive."

"You won't have to," Warrick replied. "I'll let you know exactly where to find him."

"I'll draw up the warrant," Craven muttered.

"That's a side of you I've never seen before," Warrick said as they remounted in the street.

"Not one I like to use," Philip replied. "But really. Passing it off to a different court. Imagine the bureaucracy. It could take years."

"Hopefully, they'll be ready when I send for them," Warrick said.

"Did you see their astonished faces when you told them you'd be the one to track down Watkins in the slums? Priceless!"

Warrick chuckled, determined to ignore the knot of dread tightening in his gut. He'd sworn never to return to the mean streets of Hull's dockland. There was too much of the real Warrick Farrell in those slums.

REUNION

It was a relief to find Sax still sleeping when Amelia returned to her own room. Alternately plagued by vivid memories of the terrifying ordeal and excited by Warrick's unexpected proposal, she'd spent a restless night. Her nephew, however, had slept soundly, undisturbed by nightmares—a good sign he might recover quickly.

Reluctant to wake him, she was in danger of going mad with nothing to do and no one to talk to. Getting Sax dressed, taking him downstairs for breakfast and perhaps a walk around South Ferriby would at least occupy some of the empty hours. Alex and Eliza would be well on their way but likely wouldn't arrive until much later in the day, no matter how hard their driver pushed the horses.

She was still pacing when her nephew stirred. "Good morning, Aunty Amelia," he murmured with a yawn.

"Good morning," she replied, hurrying to his bedside. "Did you have a good sleep?"

"Yes. Have my uncles left to rescue Kenny?" he asked as he sat up in bed.

Thankful for his resiliency, she could only nod, afraid her fretting might result in tears if she tried to speak.

"Don't worry," he replied. "They'll save him and get that rotter put in gaol."

"Of course," she confirmed, resolved not to cause the child any further worries. He could not be allowed to believe Watkins still posed a danger to anyone. "Now, I believe your clothes are dry. Let's get you dressed and ready for breakfast."

～

"How do you feel?" Philip asked.

Warrick stared at the cheval mirror. "Good," he lied.

The ill-shaven man dressed in dirty, tattered clothing who stared back was all too familiar—Warrick Farrell, denizen of the slums. It was as though he'd never left that life behind. "And bad," he conceded.

"I understand," Philip replied, clapping a supportive hand on his shoulder. "You don't have to do this. We can devise another way."

Warrick shook his head. "Every day we delay is another day Kenny suffers. This is the best plan."

"We'll take the curricle I keep here. I preferred not to advertise my title when I worked in Hull, so it has no crest on the door. Where do you want to be dropped off? You're liable to cause a riot if you walk through this neighborhood dressed like that."

Warrick had to concede the advice was sound. In his

ducal finery, no one would dare challenge him. It was an unassailable truth that outward appearances mattered. "The Infirmary is probably the best. I can walk from there."

Twenty minutes later, his friend shook his hand. "Send word to the townhouse," Philip said. "I'll alert the authorities as soon as I hear."

Warrick stepped out of the curricle within sight of the Royal Infirmary. Slamming the door in case anyone was watching, he made an obscene gesture as the vehicle drove off, then loped away toward the docks.

Watkins had enemies—men and women he'd bullied and brutalized over the years. Warrick hoped at least one of them would be willing to help oust the murdering thug from whatever hole he'd crawled into.

~

AT DUSK, Amelia and Sax ran out to greet the carriages when Nelthorpe announced their arrival in South Ferriby.

Alex rode alongside.

Falling to her knees in the courtyard of the inn, Eliza sobbed, unable to speak as she hugged Sax.

Tears welled in Alex's good eye as he dismounted and lifted his son into his arms.

Jenny, Rowland, Lady Penelope and Nanny Brown had traveled with them from Derbyshire, so there were hugs and tears aplenty.

Sax seemed almost embarrassed to be the center of attention, but he finally cried tears of joy when his father lifted Brutus out of the carriage. The child threw his little arms around the dog's neck. Brutus licked his face, clearly happy to be reunited with his master.

"Your son was so brave," Amelia told his parents. "He kept my spirits up when I was ready to lose hope."

Alex's chest swelled with pride as he tousled his son's hair.

Amelia explained Warrick's plan to return to the slums in order to bring Watkins to justice.

"Back to the gutter where he belongs," Lady Penelope opined.

Amelia bristled. "Warrick Farrell is one of the noblest men you could ever wish to meet, Mama," she retorted. "And you had better learn to respect my future husband."

Her sisters whooped with glee while her mother stood with her mouth agape.

"I knew it," Eliza cried, throwing her arms around Amelia and Jenny who were already hugging each other.

But it was Sax who said it best. "I'm glad Warrick will be my uncle."

The Harcourts were anxious to return straight home to Beverley on the morrow. Warrick had urged her to travel with them, but Jenny and Rowland would be going to Philip's townhouse in Hull.

Amelia was grateful when Jenny suggested she accompany her. Returning to the Harrowby Dower House to spend anxious days with her mother held no appeal. At least in the townhouse she'd be closer to Warrick while she waited for news and prayed nothing would go wrong.

UNCOUTH DUKE

~

Warrick headed for the warren of hovels in the narrow alley where he had been born and lived most of his life. It seemed fitting that a gray drizzle began as he stood at the end of the street and wrinkled his nose. He'd apparently become immune to the stench of human waste when he'd lived here. And the noise! Hungry babies wailed, drunken women screamed slurred obscenities, dogs barked, dirty urchins shouted taunts at each other.

"Welcome home," he muttered, narrowing his eyes at one of the lads scurrying by. "Peter?" he growled.

The boy paused, eyeing him. "Wot's it to ye?"

"Dost tha nay recognize me?" he said, arms spread wide. "Warrick Farrell."

Peter shook his head. "Nay. Farrell went to live wi' some posh gent."

Warrick laughed. "Is that what they say? Well, I'm free now and lookin' fer a place to lay me 'ead."

Could he help it if the lad jumped to the mistaken conclusion he'd been in gaol?

"A few of us 'ave a crib. Tha can stay there toneet if'n t'others say aye."

Afraid he might lapse all too easily into the King's English, he simply nodded and followed the urchin.

TOUGH LITTLE MEN

There were tearful goodbyes outside the inn in South Ferriby. It was the last time all the Saxton women would see each other, possibly for months. Before boarding their carriage, Eliza and Lady Penelope made a fuss about planning another ducal wedding, the latter insisting the ceremony had to take place in Beverley Minster. Amelia appreciated their efforts to take her mind off Warrick's dangerous mission, but insisted firmly that she and her future husband would be the ones to settle on the details of their marriage.

Sporting a wide grin, Sax rode to the ferry dock at New Holland in his father's lap. Amelia traveled with Jenny and Rowland in the Wentworth coach. Her nephew slept in his mother's arms as the paddle steamer made its way across the choppy Humber.

Philip welcomed them to his townhouse and brought them up to date on the legal proceedings and Warrick's departure.

Tired from the journey and worried about the man she loved, Amelia readily agreed to a nap before dinner. "Future husband," she whispered, savoring the notion when she was alone in her room. "Lady Amelia Farrell, Duchess of Beaufort."

The prospect was at once exhilarating and terrifying.

∽

Warrick was grateful to the street urchins who'd taken him in, but their brogue and bravado was a sharp reminder of how much his wards had changed. The transformation in their behavior was largely thanks to Amelia. He'd been a fool not to make her his right from the start of their relationship. His body and his heart kept telling him she was the one, but he'd steadfastly refused to listen.

If he'd provided more protection for the people he cared about, Amelia, Kenny and Sax might have been spared their long ordeal. It was a miracle Amelia still loved him after he'd insisted on marrying *well*. How could he do any better than having Amelia as his wife and the mother of his heirs? She'd carved out a place for herself in his heart, and his body had no trouble whatsoever responding to her.

An argument broke out between two of the lads, jolting him back to reality. If he hoped to return to his new life, he'd have to keep his wits about him. One wrong move would alert Watkins, and Warrick could end up as fish bait in the Humber.

However, the lads remembered him and knew he'd

sheltered orphans before his disappearance. It was only a matter of time before they tumbled to his purpose in returning to the slums. The streets had made them wise beyond their years and they would sniff out a lie. Besides, they might be useful. It was likely they steered clear of Joss Watkins' fists.

Sitting on a filthy, straw-filled mattress on the floor of a dark cellar, his knees tucked to his chest, he accepted the heel of a loaf from Peter.

"Nowt else," the lad explained.

The generosity touched Warrick's heart. The boys could easily have let him go hungry instead of sharing what little they had. "Ta," he said, tearing off a chunk of the stale bread with his teeth.

"Mind the crumbs," Peter cautioned.

Warrick nodded, having already noticed the rat droppings.

"Can I speak with yer pals?" he asked.

"Aye," Peter replied, cocking his head toward the others. They came to stand around him as if they'd been waiting for an explanation. He swallowed the lump in his throat. The scene was all too reminiscent of another quintet of tough little men, arms folded and wearing flat caps. "I've come looking fer Kenny Watkins," he confessed. "An' I need 'elp."

They eyed him cautiously, arms still folded.

"Wot's Kenny to thee?" one lad asked.

Peter answered for him. "'E's the bloke wot took Kenny in when 'is Da nigh on kilt 'im."

"Kenny's like a son to me," Warrick explained truthfully. "I took him away to start a new life, but his Pa came for him. Freddie the Ferret helped him."

"'Avn't seen 'ide nor 'air o' Freddie fer a bit," Peter said.

Warrick saw no point hiding the truth. "Watkins murdered him," he revealed. "Just before they crossed the river."

"I 'eard Watkins were back," the tallest boy offered after a long silence. "'Oled up in Bullion Street."

Warrick nodded. He knew Bullion Street well. If he went there to investigate, it was more than likely he'd bump into members of the Hull Corresponding Society, especially if they still held clandestine meetings in one of the cellars. Revolutionary unrest must still burn brightly in the hearts of Hull's working men. "I can offer a reward if you lads will keep an eye out for Watkins or Kenny."

"Wot sorta reward?" Peter asked.

"Coin," he replied, though his mind was already trying to fathom some permanent way to help these lads.

They eyed his clothing doubtfully, but he was sure they'd noticed he'd dropped the brogue.

At some unseen signal, they drifted away without another word.

Already nauseated by the stink of the hovel, Warrick got to his feet and made his way to the street. Spending the night in the boys' *crib* wasn't something he looked forward to. The place wasn't much different from where he'd lived most of his life though he'd kept his home vermin-free. The occasional cockroach he could tolerate. Rats and fleas definitely not.

Outside, he inhaled the familiar fetid odors but also a

hint of the sea. He chuckled when he realized he'd missed the salty tang in his nostrils.

Worried former acquaintances might recognize him, he pulled his cap lower, kept his head down and set off to explore some of his old haunts.

A FLAW IN THE PLAN

Wakened by the sounds of movement, Warrick stretched, amazed he'd actually slept amid the filth. There were no windows in the cellar, but a small grate high on one wall let in a sliver of light. The lads were all awake. There was no conversation between them, which didn't surprise Warrick. Children who had little to look forward to tended to be lost in thoughts of how to survive the coming day.

The tallest boy, who looked to be a year or two older than the rest, hunkered down beside Warrick's mattress. "Tha spoke o' coin," he said, a glint of uncertainty in his narrowed eyes.

"Aye," Warrick replied. "What's your name, lad?"

"Michael. Peter's bruver."

"Well, Michael. You may have heard I recently came into money. I can do more than pay you for information about Kenny Watkins."

"Like wot?"

"Better digs than this place," he replied. "Good food. Schooling if you wish."

By now, the other boys had gathered around them. Snorts of derision greeted this idea.

"Nay," Michael replied. "Schoo's nay good to us."

Warrick shook his head. "Kenny thought the same thing, but he can read and write now. That means he can expect a better life than thieving for his father and ending up in gaol, or hanging from a noose. Don't you want better things for Peter?"

"Aye. Ower da were 'ung. But mebbe tha's all talk."

"Well, when we find him, you can ask Kenny, or Eddie Powell, or Tim Cooper, or Charlie Hart or Tom Williams. They are all my wards and will vouch that I'm a man of my word."

A murmur rippled through the wide-eyed group. They'd recognized the names.

"So, wot do we 'ave to do?" Michael asked.

"When we find Kenny, someone must take a message to a friend of mine who lives on King's Terrace."

"Tha's jokin'," another boy exclaimed. "We canna go up yonder."

They were right. They'd be chased off by the rich folk who lived in that neighborhood. "You could leave a message for him at the Infirmary. Would that be possible? His name's Dr. Philip Fortescue." He deemed it preferable not to mention Philip's noble status. "Can you remember that?"

"Aye. Reet enuff," Michael replied. "Were 'im came to sign papers when Ma died o't' pox."

Warrick knew of Philip's efforts to help eradicate

smallpox. Michael and Peter had been left orphans, their parents victims of the harsh realities of slum life.

Yesterday's walk through the neighborhood had convinced him he had a duty to improve the lives of Hull's abandoned children. There were hundreds of orphans like his wards who needed someone to step in and provide assistance. He was confident Amelia would support such an endeavor. He just wished he'd had the foresight to think ahead. Expecting these urchins to go to Philip's townhouse was akin to asking them to swim the Humber.

Left alone again after the boys left, he decided to walk to the Infirmary. Philip had to be made aware of the change in plans. He no longer worked at the hospital but the authorities there would know how to contact him.

When the porter refused him admission, he realized he had an uphill battle on his hands. "I'm the Duke of Beaufort," he insisted.

"And I'm King Georgy Peorgy," the porter replied. "Now, off wi' ye."

"Dr. Fortescue won't be pleased you've turned me away. He's expecting a messenger."

Perhaps it was the *posh* accent, or maybe the mention of Philip's name that gave the porter pause. "Fortescue don't work 'ere any longer."

"It's vitally important someone take a message to his house on King's Terrace. Lives may depend on it. Tell him to meet Beaufort here at the Infirmary. The messenger will be amply rewarded."

The promise of coin banished the suspicion from the porter's eyes. Warrick had done what he could. He had to hope the message would get through. The alternative was to walk to King's Terrace and inform Philip of the change in plans, but his disguise would likely prevent him from setting foot in that neighborhood.

～

Amelia knew better than to challenge her brother-in-law directly. Philip was a forward-thinking aristocrat who'd risked his life for King and country. But he was nevertheless a man, and even enlightened men often thought they knew best.

She therefore approached her sister with the concerns that had gnawed at her all night. Philip might be more inclined to listen to his wife. Careful not to question Philip's judgement in the matter, she said, "Warrick must realize by now that his plan to send a messenger from the slums won't succeed."

Jenny's thoughtful nod came as a relief. "Expecting them to make it to King's Terrace isn't realistic."

"You and I can see that," Amelia replied.

"Because, even born into a genteel family, we wouldn't be welcome in this neighborhood if I weren't the Duchess of Wentworth."

"Exactly."

"Exactly what?" Philip asked, taking them unawares when he unexpectedly entered the drawing room.

"No one from the slums could ever hope to get all the way up here with a message," Jenny declared.

Amelia held her breath. Glad though she was that her

sister had brought up the flaw in the plan, there was no guarantee Philip would agree.

"Funny you should say that," he replied with a grin. "A courier just arrived. Jenkins at the Infirmary sent him. It seems Warrick has come to the same conclusion. I'm to await news there."

Amelia feared she might go mad isolated in King's Terrace, not knowing what was happening. But it was unlikely Philip would allow her to accompany him.

Jenny came to her rescue. "I can't go in my condition," she said coyly. "But Amelia could bring word back to me so I won't fret."

"Very well," he said with the resignation of a man who knows he's been out-maneuvered. "I'll get a curricle brought round."

THE TRAP

Michael arrived back at the cellar, his eyes wide with excitement, his younger brother tagging behind. "We found him," he explained breathlessly. "Last tenement on Bullion Street before the gasometer. Int' garret. But Watkins' bin boastin' to his pals. Ties Kenny up when he goes out at neet."

"Doesn't want his son escaping while he's out boozing," Warrick replied.

"Aye, but…"

"Our best chance to get Kenny out of there is at nighttime," Warrick supplied, forestalling the boy.

"I'll come with thee, as lookout," the lad offered.

"No. You and Peter must take word to Dr. Fortescue at the Infirmary."

"Wot if 'e ain't there?"

"He will be," Warrick replied, hoping his message had got through.

Michael scurried away.

Tempting as it was to head out immediately for Bullion Street, Warrick forced himself to wait until the shadows lengthened before setting off to free Kenny.

He'd walked these dark streets before and thought nothing of it. Now, he felt uneasy and out of his element. Perhaps the life of a wealthy duke had softened him. Or maybe he simply had more reasons to avoid danger. People depended on the success of the Beaufort dukedom. He held the power to campaign for social change. Above all, he had the love of a beautiful and intelligent woman who'd agreed to be his duchess.

These thoughts preoccupied him as he stealthily climbed the rickety stairs that clung tenuously to the outside wall of the dwelling beside the gasometer on Bullion Street.

The weathered door to the garret opened easily when he put his shoulder to it. He was relieved to see Kenny trussed up like a chicken for the pot, though the gag seemed unnecessary. "It's all right," he said softly when Kenny shook his head, tears welling in his wide eyes. "I'm going to get you out of here."

"'Ow touchin'," came an ominous reply.

Warrick spun around, raising his fists as Watkins and two beefy cronies lurched toward him. He'd walked straight into the trap.

~

Lady Penelope always claimed she had a sixth sense. Amelia wondered if perhaps she'd inherited her mother's ability to know deep down when something had gone wrong. She couldn't rid herself of the ball of dread lodged in her belly. Warrick had confessed that he'd hurried back from London because he'd had a premonition something untoward had happened to her. Was it love that alerted you when your beloved was in danger?

"Warrick's in trouble," she told Philip for probably the umpteenth time.

"I've sent word to the High Sherrif to call out the Night Watch," he replied, obviously equally concerned. "They'll meet us at the Infirmary."

When they arrived, they found three constables manhandling two scruffy boys. The smaller of the two was pummeling the legs of a six-foot-tall giant who held the other boy by the ear. Amelia immediately recognized the flat caps. These were the kind of lads who would gravitate to Warrick. "They're the messengers," she exclaimed.

Philip jumped from the curricle and demanded to know what was happening.

"These good-for-nothings want to speak to a doctor," the man holding the older boy sneered.

"I'm Dr. Fortescue," he said to the lads. "Is it me you've come to see?"

"Aye," the boy groused, sticking out his tongue at the watchman. "Warrick said to tell thee 'es gone to rescue Kenny."

"At night?"

"Best time. His Da ties 'im up in a garret while he guz owt."

Amelia's throat constricted. It sounded too easy.

"I don't like this," Philip said. "Give me the directions."

"With me," he shouted to the watchmen after learning the address. "The far end of Bullion Street."

Grumbling and hesitation greeted this command.

"I'm the Duke of Wentworth," Philip shouted more loudly. "I'll see any man punished who fails in his duty to save lives this night."

The grumbling ceased.

"Take these two heroes inside," he said, turning to Amelia. "Tell the nurses I sent you. I promise to bring Warrick and Kenny out safely."

The Watchmen loped off, billy-clubs in hand and lanterns held high, leaving Amelia with no alternative but to usher the urchins into the hospital. She uttered a silent prayer of thanks she and Philip had arrived before the messengers had been sent packing.

"'Ope they get there in time," the older boy said. "It's nigh on two mile to Bullion Street."

"Warrick promised us coin," his freckle-faced sidekick said. "And more."

Amelia swallowed the lump in her throat. It was typically generous of Warrick to want to help these underprivileged children. "Well, he's a man of his word," she replied. "Now, let's see if we can find you something to eat."

~

Warrick opened his eyes, quickly closing them again when pain arrowed through his skull. He inhaled deeply, then wished he hadn't.

"Broken ribs, probly."

Tentatively, Warrick opened one eye, the memory of the beating rushing back when he saw Kenny. The boy's gag had been removed, but he was still tied to the rusted bed-frame. "You could be right," he conceded, discovering when he tried to move that his hands and feet were tied.

"Thanks for coming for me," Kenny said. "I 'oped tha' would, but I'm sorry...for everything."

"Not your fault," Warrick wheezed, fighting dizziness. "Where's your father?"

"Celebratin' with his pals," Kenny replied with disgust. "Nay doubt three sheets to the wind by now."

"We have to be gone by the time he returns," Warrick declared.

"And 'ow will we manage that?"

"Don't you know a crafty slum dweller never goes anywhere without a dagger in his boot?"

He made an agonizing attempt to reach the knife, suspecting a broken rib had pierced his lung. "You'll have to get it," he rasped, edging closer to Kenny.

Hampered by his bonds, the boy strained for endless minutes to reach the weapon, finally grasping it with both hands.

"Free yourself first," Warrick said.

He drifted in and out of consciousness, too weak to offer encouragement while Kenny sawed at the ropes binding him.

He had no idea how much time had passed when he realized his hands and feet were free. "Thanks," he growled groggily, afraid he might swoon when Kenny tried to help him rise.

"We 'ave to get out of 'ere, Beaufort," Kenny growled. "I smell smoke."

TEACAKES AND LEMONADE

As Philip and a group of younger constables rushed to the end of Bullion Street, he became keenly aware of two things. Firstly, wisps of smoke drifted from an upper story and, secondly, one of the beefy fellows lumbering down the outer stairs looked remarkably like the brute who'd thrown Sax overboard.

The older watchmen would eventually catch up but, if the fire took hold, the whole street would go up in flames. Philip had to act now. There was no sign of Warrick or Kenny among the disgruntled group already milling about in the street, so he had to assume they were still in the garret. Pointing to Watkins and his cronies, he shouted to the constables, "Apprehend the firebrands when they get to the bottom."

He watched in horror as the crowd reacted to his command. They swarmed Watkins and his bully-boys, dragging them off the staircase before the constables could reach them. He supposed he could understand their desperate anger. Fire would destroy their meager lives.

Pushing his way through the throng, he reached the last step and looked up to see Kenny and Warrick. But something was wrong. Warrick gripped the flimsy railing while Kenny struggled to keep him upright. Clearly, they were in no position to douse the fire.

"We need water up there. Now!" he screamed at the top of his lungs, hoping his voice might penetrate the bloodlust. He vaulted up the stairs, not sure if the pounding in his ears was his own heartbeat or the footsteps of men following behind.

∽

Gritting his teeth against the pain, Warrick gripped the railing and tried to disentangle himself from Kenny's grip. "Save yourself," he urged.

"Not a chance, Beaufort," the boy replied. "You didn't abandon me."

Warrick thought he must be delirious when a breathless Philip suddenly appeared, put a hand on his shoulder and choked out his name.

"Inside," Kenny explained. "Old rugs and such. More smoke than fire."

Warrick swayed, narrowing his eyes when more men rushed past him and entered the garret behind Philip. He could have sworn water sloshed out of the buckets they carried, but that was impossible.

"Careful," Kenny warned as he guided Warrick to the first stair. "The steps are wet."

If only breathing wasn't so painful, Warrick might be able to grasp what was going on.

"Half way," Kenny said after an eternity.

"Fire's out!"

He thought it was Philip's voice, but looking up was risky.

A loud cheer resounded from the street below. Strong hands reached to help him as he struggled to remain upright.

"Tha's safe now," someone said.

Warrick nodded and let the darkness claim him as his knees buckled.

∾

AMELIA SAT on a bench near the Infirmary's main entrance with an arm around each sleeping urchin. She'd listened to their enthusiastic chatter about the food she'd procured for them. The country was in a sorry state when stale teacakes and watery lemonade constituted a feast for two little boys. Then, suddenly, it was as if a candle had been snuffed out. They'd cuddled into her and fallen asleep. She couldn't stop yawning, but a compulsion to watch the door kept her awake.

Minutes, or perhaps hours later, urgent voices and movement jolted her from a doze. She could scarcely believe she'd nodded off, but guilt was forgotten when two stretcher-bearers hurried in. Their patient's eyes were swollen shut, his face battered and bruised. He was almost unrecognizable, but her broken heart knew it was Warrick. She took hold of his hand and lifted it to her trembling lips, nigh on falling to her knees with gratitude when he smiled and rasped, "Amelia."

Philip took hold of her arm as they carried Warrick away. "He's been badly beaten, but we got Kenny out. I'll keep you informed."

With that he was gone.

Through her tears, she saw Kenny standing nearby, looking uncertain. He ran into her embrace when she opened her arms. Sobbing, they clung to each other until Peter nudged Kenny and asked, "Want a teacake?"

∼

WARRICK HEARD PHILIP'S VOICE, but couldn't understand what he was saying. When he tried to reply, his tongue felt too big for his mouth. However, he was grateful for whatever drug they'd used to relieve his pain, and the only thing that truly mattered was feeling Amelia's firm grip on his hand whenever he drifted back to the world. She was the anchor that kept hope alive.

"How long?" he finally managed.

"A day and a half," Philip replied. "I'd like to move you to my home now you're on the mend."

"Moving sounds painful," he admitted.

"It might be uncomfortable," his friend agreed. "Your lung was punctured by a broken rib, so you'll have to be careful not to exert yourself."

"Wouldn't it be better for him to stay here?" Amelia asked, meshing her fingers with his.

"I have to be honest with you," Philip replied. "I worked hard to improve things here. The Infirmary employs an excellent Bug Catcher whose job it is to rid the mattresses of lice. Indeed, he's paid more than the surgeons."

Warrick immediately felt itchy all over.

Amelia sighed. "When I was in Bolton, I heard of a patient who found mushrooms and maggots in his bed linens. They call the hospital the *House of Death*."

"Unfortunately," Philip added. "Some hospitals are breeding grounds for fevers. Here, there is no ventilation and fresh air's what you need."

"I don't care where I am," Warrick replied. "So long as Amelia is there."

"I'll see to the arrangements," Philip declared.

CONVALESCING

Philip hired a nurse to take care of Warrick once he was transported to the Hull townhouse.

With growing impatience, Amelia tolerated two days of being asked by the officious woman to leave the chamber while she gave His Grace a bed bath, or administered his dose of laudanum, or changed his bandages.

"I should be taking care of my betrothed," she complained to Jenny.

"You help to feed him," her sister replied.

"I mean...er...other things, to do with his care."

"Sounds like you're jealous."

"What if I am?" she retorted.

"I'll speak to Philip," Jenny promised. "He'll know what's for the best."

Tempted to reply that Warrick would heal faster under her loving care, Amelia bit her tongue. Later that afternoon, she was glad she had kept quiet when Philip instructed the nurse to explain the necessary procedures to her.

How to administer just the right amount of laudanum was easy to understand and carry out. Giving Warrick a sponge bath under the critical eye of the nurse threatened to be overwhelming. She'd always known he was a well built man, but she became overheated simply cleansing his bare arms. His broad chest was heavily bandaged, so, for now, she was spared the necessity of attending to that part of his anatomy. There were bruises enough on his torso. Sponging droplets of water off the line of dark hair that meandered down his flat belly caused an ache to blossom in a very private place.

The lustful glint in Warrick's eyes didn't help her equilibrium, nor did the nurse's frequent mutterings that none of this was *proper*.

Long legs hidden beneath the linens had yet to be tackled. "Amelia's to be my wife," he told the nurse, grinning as he kicked off the sheet. "I'm not embarrassed for her to see me at my worst."

An urge to smooth her fingertips over the dark hair on powerful thighs gripped Amelia. But it was the lance jutting proudly from its nest of dark curls that held her gaze. She'd known men were made differently but, if this was Warrick at his worst...

The indignant nurse fled.

Eyes narrowed, Warrick laughed seductively as he grasped Amelia's hand and curled it around his manhood. "See what your loving touch does to me? My cock salutes you, lass," he said.

He watched her carefully, no doubt to gauge her reaction. The prim and proper Amelia Saxton should have fled with the nurse. But this was the rough and ready side of Warrick that tugged at her heartstrings and other, more intimate parts of her body. She returned his smile and slowly stroked his impressive *cock* with the sponge.

"I feel better already," he growled.

"So do I," she confessed.

~

"Your recovery has been nothing short of miraculous," Philip observed on the fifth morning after the rescue.

Warrick noted a hint of amusement in the comment. His host must suspect his growing intimacy with Amelia, but neither he nor his duchess had voiced any objection to her role as his *nurse*. The real nurse must have declared her outrage when she abruptly gave notice, but Philip had simply smiled knowingly when he brought the news.

Warrick's explorations of Amelia's intimate places had helped his body heal faster. Watching her first sexual release had humbled and strengthened him. Her little nubbin was so very responsive. He longed to taste her juices. Her obvious appreciation for his male endowments was arousing to say the least. She wasn't at all shocked when her small hands caused his seed to erupt with more force than he ever thought possible. He grew increasingly impatient to join his body to hers. But there was no necessity for anyone else to learn of the delights they shared. Let them suspect, if they wished. Warrick certainly wasn't going to betray his beloved's trust.

However, his respect and gratitude for Philip's friendship was growing into something deeper. Philip had saved his life but there was more to it than that. A sense of male camaraderie had developed between them. Despite his admittedly un-duke like behavior in the privacy of the sick room, Warrick felt less of an outsider looking in.

Ironically, Amelia the commoner was the key that had allowed him entry into the private world of a genuine friendship between titled gentlemen.

"How long before I can take Amelia home to Cavendish?" he asked.

"Let's get you out of bed today and see how you feel by supper time."

∽

"I sense Kenny is anxious to leave Hull," Amelia told Warrick when she joined him and Philip that same morning. "He's waiting to speak to you."

"Good," he replied. "Philip says I can get out of bed, and I have a feeling he might need help getting me up."

It was tempting to coyly tease that she usually had no trouble in that regard, but Philip would think less of her—although, come to think on it, Jenny had made a few cryptic comments...

Shaking her head to dispel the disquieting vision of her sister in bed with Philip, she opened the door to invite Kenny in. He'd been to visit Warrick every day but, on this occasion, the absence of his flat cap suggested something was afoot.

"Beaufort," the lad began without a trace of the brogue. "How are you today?"

"Better. And Wentworth says I can get out of bed, so I need your strong arm to assist."

Warrick's tight grimace betrayed his continued discomfort getting into a sitting position, but breathing had become easier, a sign his lung was on the mend. He carefully swung his legs over the side of the bed and planted his feet on the carpeted floor. "Let's hope for the best," he said as Kenny took hold of one arm, Philip the other.

Standing proved easier than anyone expected, but he swayed on his feet.

"Dizzy," he confessed.

"Take your time," Philip cautioned. "Don't expect to do too much at first."

"I feel like a weakling."

"You suffered serious injuries. Your body has to relearn how to do things that came naturally before."

Amelia had to look away when Warrick winked at her. Certain parts of his anatomy had performed admirably.

"Try a few steps," Philip suggested. "We'll hold on until you feel steady."

"It's a pity Eliza isn't here to help," Amelia said, feeling hopeful when Warrick eventually managed a few steps on his own. "Her Swedish exercises and massage did wonders for her husband. Alex still swears by them."

The heat rose in her face when Warrick replied,

"You'll have to get her to teach you how to effectively massage my aches and pains."

She expected Philip to be shocked, but he laughed heartily and said, "You'll have your hands full with this one."

Surely this was inappropriate banter for a young boy to hear. A quick glance at Kenny showed him chewing his bottom lip, clearly preoccupied.

She'd told Warrick of the boy's bravery and his protection of Sax during the ordeal with Watkins. He'd shared Kenny's refusal to abandon him in the burning garret.

They agreed the swaggering adolescent had discovered a fortitude he perhaps didn't know he had and was becoming a man.

"That's enough for now," Warrick rasped. "I'll sit for a bit."

"I'll be off," Philip said once Warrick was settled in a chair by the hearth.

Kenny dithered, seemingly unsure whether to stay or leave with Philip.

"Something's troubling you," Amelia said, suspecting it might be the recent news that his father's body had been found floating in the Humber.

"I've a boon to ask," Kenny replied, his jaw clenched.

"If it's in my power, I'll grant it," Warrick assured him.

"I no longer want to be called Kenny."

Amelia exchanged a puzzled glance with Warrick.

The lad shifted his weight. "Kenneth is more...er..."

"Grown up?" Amelia supplied.

"Good idea," Warrick agreed. "You've proven you're not a child any more, young man. Kenneth it is."

The two shook hands and Kenneth Watkins left with bare head held high.

Homeward Bound

By the tenth day of his convalescence, Warrick was declared fit enough to travel home. He'd already dined at Wentworth's table for several days and wanted to take the opportunity of this last night with his friends to discuss a matter of importance.

"Coming back to the slums has forced me to see that there are hundreds of lads who need help."

"Boys like Michael and Peter," Amelia said.

"And Kenny. Sorry, Kenneth," Warrick added with a smile.

Kenneth returned the smile, aware he was being teased.

"What they need is a school," Philip suggested.

"And Amelia as their teacher," Jenny added.

"Absolutely not," Warrick replied. "Amelia's going to have her hands full teaching me how to be a proper duke. But you're right about the school."

"They need more than that," Kenneth interjected.

"What's the use of going to school during the day then having to return home to some hovel?"

"And exposure to all the dangers of the slums," Philip agreed.

"It would have to be a boarding school," Amelia said, voicing Warrick's thoughts.

"A school that fed and clothed them and offered a safe haven as well as an education," he said.

"But how do they pay for all this?" Kenneth asked.

"They don't. I foot the bill," Warrick declared, trusting Amelia would support the plan.

She linked her arm with his. "I'm so proud of you," she whispered.

The swell of her breast against his bicep threatened to distract him but he marshaled his thoughts when Philip shook his head. "We can't allow you to take on all the responsibility. You'll need a location and this house will be empty when Jenny and I return home to Lincolnshire. How about a lease? Say two pounds sterling per annum."

Warrick recognized the magnificent townhouse was worth much more. "Your neighbors might object," he warned.

"Well, we'll follow Alex and Eliza's lead and give it a prestigious name and solicit people from the neighborhood to sit on the board," Jenny suggested.

Philip's eyes lit up. "I'm positive Alex would be only too glad to contribute since he lives in this county and not too far from Hull."

"Harrowby would be perfect as chairman of the board," Warrick declared.

"So," Amelia said. "What name shall we choose?"

~

Amelia, Warrick and Kenneth spent the first hour of the journey home discussing possible names for the proposed school. Warrick was enthusiastic about the plans they'd made to correspond with the Harcourts and Fortescues concerning the establishment of the school.

However, Amelia could see the jostling was taking a toll on his still-healing ribs and was glad when the laudanum he'd reluctantly agreed to swallow took effect and he dozed off.

Philip had prescribed a few days rest once they arrived back at Cavendish Manor, but Amelia suspected Warrick would instead throw his energy into hiring staff, constituting a board, recruiting pupils and so on.

She was eager to assist in the noble endeavor, confident he would solicit her help.

As the miles sped by, her eyelids drooped. Lulled by the rhythmic beat of the horses' hooves, her mind drifted to the events of the past few years. So many unlikely things had happened to her family. If her dear Papa hadn't sent Eliza abroad to study the medical benefits of Swedish exercise and massage, Alex Harcourt would never have met and married Amelia's older sister. Then Jenny would not have met Philip, since it was Philip who'd persuaded Alex to accept Eliza's help. And if James Hastings hadn't decided to name Warrick as his heir, the man she loved...

A bump in the road jolted her awake. She hoped she

hadn't drooled when she realized Kenneth was watching her.

"I was just thinking," he said, leaning forward. "Beaufort's always been a noble chap."

Still half asleep, she nodded.

"Even before he became a duke, he took me and the lads in. Gave my Da a good beating when he came to drag me back once before."

She nodded again.

"I'm glad you see that side of him, Miss Saxton."

Her breath hitched. Love for Warrick shone in his eyes. "I do, and I promise I'll be a good wife."

"He's lucky to have found you."

The young man settled back into his corner of the carriage. Amelia was obliged to revisit her previous thoughts about relationships. Was it luck that brought people who loved each other together? Or was it all part of God's plan?

∼

WARRICK OPENED ONE EYE, pleased to see Amelia had fallen back to sleep. Or perhaps, like him, she'd never really slept. The small dose of laudanum had helped dull the pain in his ribs, but he'd only dozed.

He chuckled inwardly. The street-wise Kenny Watkins was an unlikely person to inspire fatherly feelings, but Kenneth's words served as a sharp reminder to pursue legal guardianship of his lads. Their future had seemed uncertain until Amelia's arrival. Now, he saw the potential for them to do well in life.

The temptation to take Amelia into his arms was powerful, though his bandaged ribs might protest. He doubted Kenneth would be shocked, or later boast of the improper behavior he'd been privy to.

Still, Amelia would be embarrassed. He liked that she projected a *proper* image to the outside world, whereas he'd come to know the wild, unfettered woman who lurked within. He suspected she'd allowed him to see that side of her because she recognized they weren't so different. Anticipating years of sexual abandon, he shifted in his seat to relieve the pressure building in his eager cock.

COMING CLEAN

It seemed to Amelia that every person who lived at Cavendish Manor hurried out to the courtyard to welcome them home. Messages had been sent informing the staff of the need to remain in Hull for a few days, though Warrick hadn't wanted to explain the reasons. He didn't want the lads worrying about him.

"It's good to see you safely returned, Your Grace," Wilson said, looking relieved. "And Miss Saxton, of course. And Master Kenny."

His eyes widened when the latter extended a hand. "It's Kenneth now, Mr. Wilson, and I'd like to apologize for my previous behavior. I can assure you there'll be no more trouble from this lot."

The butler accepted the handshake, but turned a puzzled frown on a smiling Warrick who merely nodded.

The boys included in Kenneth's sweeping gesture gaped at him, but the note of authority in their friend's voice had them nodding their agreement.

Looking sheepish, Tim and Tom stepped forward.

"We're sorry, Kenny," Tim said. "We feared yer Da would kill us if we told on 'im."

"It's Kenneth from now on," he replied, hunkering down. "I don't blame you. He terrified me too, until I realized he had no power over me if I didn't show fear."

Tim and Tom's frowns indicated to Amelia that they didn't fully understand. "I think Kenneth is trying to say that you can't let a bully see you're afraid of him. He feeds on fear."

"Let's get inside," Warrick said. "I'm anxious for a good soak in the tub."

Wilson raised an eyebrow, no doubt of the opinion such a declaration was unsuitable for the ears of a gently bred young lady. "Of course, Your Grace," he said.

Amelia felt smug. Little did the butler suspect.

"By the by," Warrick added. "Miss Saxton and I are betrothed. She's consented to be my bride."

The next thing Amelia knew, the cheering lads were clinging to her skirts. Every servant, including Wilson, was congratulating Warrick on his good fortune. Her heart rejoiced. She was exactly where she belonged.

~

Warrick lay his head back against the wooden bathtub. "You'll be horrified to hear I never took a bath when I lived in dockland."

"Why would that surprise me?" Amelia replied, soaping up a flannel. "Preparing a bath was hard enough in our little family cottage in Beverley."

Speaking of hard, Warrick's cock was already at full

salute in anticipation of what Amelia intended with the soapy cloth. "Now, I'm addicted to bathing," he said, taking hold of her wrist. "Especially when I have you to wash away the cares of the day."

"Careful," she cautioned with a seductive smile. "You'll get me wet."

The rigid nipples poking at her damp bodice raised the possibility her secret place was already wet. He decided to take a risk. "Then remove your clothes and join me."

Amelia the Governess hesitated, but she couldn't hide the wanton glint in her eyes. "Perhaps my gown," she allowed. "Just so it doesn't get soaked."

She turned her back and perched on the edge of the tub so he could untie the laces, then shimmied out of the frock.

Ripe breasts nigh on overflowed a beautifully embroidered corset. If she bent over slightly, he'd wager rosy nipples would put in an appearance. Every drop of saliva left his mouth. He'd let himself in for a world of frustration. But his rampant cock didn't care. "Petticoats, too," he said.

The underskirts were removed without argument, leaving her standing before him in corset, hose and garters. They'd touched each other intimately but never actually removed clothing. His cock throbbed with admiration. Ravenous to get his mouth on those eager nipples, he stood, reached over and pulled her into the tub.

Water sloshed over the side when he sat with her in his arms. She opened her mouth to protest, but he held her tight and stifled her objections with a kiss. When she calmed, he glanced down, gratified to see pouting nipples bared to his gaze. "I forget how to behave properly sometimes," he admitted, licking a nipple.

"Naughty man," she breathed, sifting her fingers through his wet hair when he suckled hard.

If she thought he was being naughty now...

~

AMELIA SURRENDERED to the intoxicating sensations spiraling through her body. She didn't care if society frowned on this sort of behavior. Warrick was a man who set his own rules and she would happily follow where he led—as evidenced by her being scantily clad in a bathtub with a man.

The reasons she allowed him to take liberties were simple. She trusted that he would never hurt her, and life with him promised to be fun, exciting and full of surprises.

She squealed when he stood unexpectedly. The bruises were almost gone. Water rolled off his lean, well-muscled body. He was Poseidon rising from the waves, his manhood jutting proudly. Seized by an irresistible urge, she shook her head when he tried to lift her from her knees. "Let me taste you," she whispered.

"Amelia," he rasped in reply as his gaze darkened.

She curled a hand around his thick length, licked the tip, then took him into her mouth.

He tasted soapy, but something else stole up her nostrils, something uniquely male.

"You've no idea how I long to be inside you," he growled, holding her head as she suckled.

"I want to be yours," she replied, her inner muscles clenching on the quivering ache blossoming in her sheath.

"You're already mine," he said. "But I won't take your virginity until we marry. We both have a right to that. Now, you'd best stop or I'll come in your mouth."

~

The boys were anxious to hear the whole story of the kidnapping and rescue, so Warrick gathered them in the schoolroom the next day after breakfast and instructed Kenneth to begin with his part of the tale.

The boy recounted the horrors of the five day trek across three counties, attributing everyone's survival to Amelia's fortitude and Sax's courage. "I couldn't have made it without them," he insisted.

Amelia shook her head. "I agree with Kenneth about my nephew's courage. He never cried once. I'm not ashamed to admit that I did cry—often."

"We don't blame you, Miss," Eddie said.

"But," she continued, "I was inspired not to lose hope because I saw Kenneth summon his courage. I knew I couldn't save us by myself, but with Kenneth's help..."

"Nay, Miss Saxton," Kenneth interjected. "It was my fault my father threw you and Sax in the Humber."

There was a collective gasp from the audience.

"Nonsense," she replied. "You sacrificed your own freedom so we could be rescued."

Confused gazes looked up at her. "His Grace pulled me from the river," she explained. "The Duke of Wentworth saved Sax. However, in the meantime, Watkins made his getaway across the river with Kenneth."

"It's like the book you read to us, Miss Saxton," Charlie exclaimed. "Except Beaufort's the hero, not Sir Ivanhoe."

"So, how come Kenneth's here?" Tom asked.

"Because," Kenneth replied. "Like a hero, His Grace refused to give up. He came to get me."

"Yes, well," Warrick said, embarrassed to be thought of as heroic. "That didn't go according to plan. I stupidly walked into a trap, and Kenneth ended up saving me. He's the true hero."

"Cor!" Eddie exclaimed. "You should write a book about it, Miss Saxton."

"Maybe I will," she said.

PREPARING FOR THE BIG DAY

When the Mawdsley brothers delivered the writ of guardianship, the elder brother was only too pleased to be asked to read the provisions out loud for His Grace.

Amelia hid a smile when Warrick asked for an explanation of this clause or the other. His reading skills had improved enormously. She was quite certain none of the legal gentlemen suspected he needed their help to understand some of the wording.

But her true pride lay in her fiancé's incredible generosity. He'd provided an annuity of one hundred pounds for each boy, payable on his coming of age.

Archibald Mawdsley also accompanied Warrick to visit the Bishop of Southwell in Nottingham in order to obtain a special license for their marriage. He and Amelia trusted Archibald to make sure everything detail of the license was in order before it was presented to the minister at St. Werburgh's in Derby.

Amelia dashed off letters to her family as soon as the date for the wedding was agreed upon with the minister.

Predictably, her mother's reply was full of outrage that they hadn't chosen Beverley Minster. Eliza and Jenny wrote to express their delight and assured her they'd be there despite both being heavily pregnant.

"With all of us gathered in one place," Warrick said, "We should be able to make good progress with plans for the school."

She too was glad of the opportunity to firm up the plans, but hoped the establishment of the charity wouldn't overshadow their special day.

Excitement for the upcoming nuptials was high among the staff of Cavendish Manor. Even the housekeeper seemed happy, though she must be aware that her master and future mistress often shared the bathtub. It was good to hear Carlos singing loudly in his native language. He'd been eerily subdued after his beating and still walked with the aid of a cane.

Warrick's wards behaved like perfect gentlemen, especially after they were informed they'd be an important part of the bridegroom's entourage. Kenneth had always been the acknowledged leader of the group. Since his return, he'd taken on the role of chief disciplinarian. Any hint of misbehavior was immediately rebuked.

Amelia feared perhaps he was becoming too harsh a taskmaster. "Sometimes, little boys have to misbehave," she told Warrick.

"Big boys too," he replied, grinning seductively. "He'll ease off once he gets over his guilt."

His remark gave her pause. "Should I feel guilty that you and I...?"

He narrowed his eyes. "Have done what? Learned to pleasure each other and will get even better at it? There's nothing sinful in that."

"I only ask because I don't feel the least bit guilty," she assured him. "I never thought much about sexual excitement until I met you. Now, I crave your touch constantly."

He took her into his embrace. "And the best is yet to come, my love."

∽

Two days before the ceremony, Kenneth was visibly disappointed when Sax didn't arrive with his parents and grandmother. Warrick intended to speak to him later about it, but Alex Harcourt approached the lad shortly after handing down his very pregnant wife from the carriage. "My duchess and I want to thank you personally for what you did to protect our son," Alex said, extending a hand. "Sax never stops talking about you and was most indignant when we told him he'd have to stay home with Nanny Brown on this trip."

Kenneth squared his shoulders and returned the handshake. "He's a grand lad, Your Grace."

"Indeed," Alex affirmed, perhaps slightly amused at having the future Duke of Harrowby referred to as a *grand lad*.

"If you ever return to Yorkshire, you can visit us at

Harrowby Hall," Eliza said, her arm linked with Amelia's. "Sax would love that."

"I'd be honored," Kenneth replied. "Though Yorkshire doesn't hold good memories for me."

"No," Alex said, flipping up the patch covering his glass eye. "I understand how you feel. But, I know first hand that time will heal the wounds."

Warrick clenched his jaw, grateful to Alex for sharing a glimpse into his journey from hellish despair to happiness. A loud cough drew his attention to Lady Penelope standing beside him.

"Well?" she asked. "Is my future son-in-law going to escort me into the house?"

He was about to offer his arm when the Wentworth carriage rolled into the avenue. Another ten minutes of squeals and hugs ensued. The Fortescues had left Rowland at home. After being pried from the coach, Jenny waddled about like a duck.

"Good grief," Amelia whispered to Warrick. "My sister looks like she might deliver any day."

Warrick suddenly felt queasy.

~

"I know you're all just family," Amelia said, grateful for Warrick's hand at the small of her back as she rose to propose a toast.

"What do you mean? *Just* family," Eliza quipped.

Teasing laughter followed.

Amelia cleared her throat and began again. "I feel I am hosting my first dinner party as Duchess of Beaufort, and I am thrilled our wards and my family are my guests." She raised her glass. "Thank you all for coming."

"Wouldn't have missed it for the world," echoed around the table as everyone except the expectant mothers and the lads drank the sweet wine.

When Amelia sat, Alex came to his feet. "It falls to me as the first to marry into the Saxton family, to salute Beaufort as the newest member of our tribe."

"Beaufort," everyone shouted good-naturedly as they raised their glasses.

Amelia sensed Warrick's turmoil as he stood with jaw clenched.

"Forgive me if I get emotional," he said hoarsely. "Sometimes, I can scarcely believe the good fortune that has befallen me."

Amelia choked back tears as her guests nodded.

"Not only am I now a titled gentleman..."

Smiles all round.

"...I have been blessed with Amelia Saxton as my bride. I love her more than life, not only because she is beautiful, intelligent and will make the perfect duchess —I know this thanks to the two duchesses here tonight —but also because she has brought me into the fold of the first real family I've ever had."

A poignant silence reigned until Jenny exclaimed, "Oh, dear."

⁓

WARRICK HAD INTENDED to ask Philip to act as his best man, but that idea disappeared like a puff of smoke the moment his friend carried Jenny out of the dining room after her labor began.

The midwife was summoned.

Amelia and Lady Penelope were dragooned into assisting the appropriately named Mrs. Brest.

Philip was banished from his wife's bedside.

The lads were eventually sent to bed when midnight came and there'd been no end to the faint screams from upstairs.

When Eliza finally agreed to retire in the wee small hours of the morning, only Warrick, Alex and Philip sipped brandy in the study.

Alex had offered to escort Amelia down the aisle, so Warrick couldn't ask him to be best man, although he'd done double duty at Philip's wedding.

"Why don't you ask Kenneth?" Alex suggested, apparently sensing Warrick's dilemma.

It was such an obvious choice, Warrick couldn't imagine why he hadn't thought of it before. Some people might be offended by his choice of a former street urchin—Lady Penelope sprang to mind—but he and Kenneth had a shared history that went back a long way. "I'll ask him. It's a good idea."

"It never gets any easier," Philip muttered some time later.

Half asleep, Warrick wasn't sure what he'd missed.

"The waiting. This is our second child but I'm even more terrified than I was with Rowland."

"I know what you mean," Alex replied. "This will be Eliza's third confinement and I'll be a wreck. The thought of losing her..."

Warrick understood why his friend couldn't voice his worst fear. One day, he'd be the one anxiously awaiting news of the birth of his first child. The prospect was at once thrilling and terrifying. Death in childbirth was an everyday occurrence in the slums, but wealth didn't guarantee tragedy wouldn't strike. He could only pray his Amelia would be safely delivered of many healthy children.

※

Exhausted and overwhelmed by a thousand and one thoughts rushing through her brain, Amelia absently stroked the dusting of fair hair on her newborn niece's head.

"She's perfect," Jenny whispered. "Wait until your daddy sees you, little one."

Her sister's labor had been an eye-opening experience for Amelia. She couldn't understand why Jenny looked so radiantly happy after screaming blue murder for ten hours. And the blood! It was enough to put a girl off having children at all—except... "She has such tiny toes," she exclaimed.

"Definitely takes after me," Lady Penelope said wearily, looking more disheveled than Jenny.

Amelia was too tired to voice the hope that wasn't a prophetic statement.

"Your Grace," Mrs. Brest declared as a haggard Philip burst into the chamber, his eyes bloodshot, his hair a rat's nest.

Ignoring the midwife's protests, he went straight to

the bed and lifted the babe from his smiling wife's arms. "My little girl," he cooed, rocking the child. "My daughter."

Closing her eyes, Amelia swallowed the lump in her throat. In her mind's eye, she saw Warrick cradling their babe, ecstatically happy and proud. A strong giant gently rocking a tiny new life.

Sensing Philip and Jenny should be left alone to enjoy their daughter, Amelia struggled to remember what she was supposed to be doing today.

She was relieved to encounter a bleary-eyed Warrick on the landing outside the chamber. No doubt he'd been up all night too. Perhaps they could take a long nap together.

"Your dressmaker and her seamstress have arrived," he said.

Then she remembered. "Oh, Lord. The last fitting. I'm getting married tomorrow."

A WEDDING

S tanding before the altar of St. Werburgh's with Kenneth at his side, Warrick's recollection of the previous day remained blurred.

He recalled visiting the local tailor's shop with Kenneth and being told the production of a suitable suit of clothes in one day was impossible. Nevertheless, garbed like an affluent young man of means, his best man wore an impressive made-to-measure three piece. Warrick discovered that imitating Philip's feigned aristocratic hauteur could work wonders. However, the promise of a reserved seat in the front pews for the tailor and his family had also helped carry the day. *Wedding of the century* might have been something of an exaggeration, but the tailor had seized the opportunity. At least it meant there was somebody beside his wards seated on Warrick's side of the church.

He exchanged a brief smile with his best man. He'd thought Kenneth was going to fall at his feet when he'd asked him, but then the young man squared his shoulders and declared, "It's an honor, Your Grace. You can count on me." He had a feeling he'd always be able to count on Kenneth Watkins and was very glad he'd chosen him as his best man.

"Best of British."

Philip?

Warrick turned to see Philip escort Lady Penelope into the front pew, the outrageous feathers of her hat drawing everyone's gaze. As far as he knew, there were no peacocks on Cavendish lands. He nodded his thanks for the good wishes, astonished and grateful his friend had torn himself away from his wife and newborn child to attend this ceremony.

It was amazing how the unexpected, early arrival of a babe could throw a relatively orderly household into chaos. Everyone seemed to be in a hurry to go somewhere or do something. Mrs. Knight remembered an old bassinet in the attic which Wilson retrieved with help from Tim and Tom. Carlos formally presented Philip with a silver medallion of his patron saint. "For *la niña*, when she grows," he said, reverently kissing the medallion before handing it over.

And Amelia had been everywhere at once. She'd been fitted for her wedding gown, reviewed arrangements for the banquet with the cook and her helpers, rearranged the seating plan, supervised the placement of flowers brought from a local greenhouse to decorate the dining room, cut up towels to serve as nappies, forced Jenny to consume a bowl of broth when she insisted she wasn't hungry, ordered Eliza to put her feet up for an hour because they certainly didn't need another baby today, and been strangely preoccupied when she returned from watching Jenny breast feed the babe. All in all, she'd left him breathless.

He struggled to get air into his lungs, the events of yesterday forgotten, when the organist launched into the appropriate music and he and Kenneth turned to greet his bride.

∾

IN THE ODD way a person knows there are seemingly unimportant details of a milestone event they will forever remember, the cadence of Alex's limp would have a permanent place in Amelia's mind. He set the perfect dignified pace as he escorted her up the aisle.

A puzzled murmur wafted its way through the congregation packed into the church. Most locals had likely never seen the Duke of Harrowby before. It was amusing to think the presence of this dignified man with the eyepatch would likely provide more fodder for local gossip than the event itself. And a pregnant woman trailing behind as the maid of honor! Apparently the bride's sister was a duchess!

She blinked when they reached the front pews. Were those tears of approval brimming in her mother's eyes?

But the most vivid memory would be the admiration in Warrick's gaze as Alex passed her hand into his.

All the frantic chaos of the previous day melted away. Apart from Jenny's absence, everything was as it should be. Amelia was marrying the man she loved who loved her in return.

The organist played. The choir sang. The minister preached at undue length and then spoke the time-honored words. She and Warrick made the traditional vows, though they both knew the ceremony was simply a formality, necessary for official recognition of their union. The love and respect they shared went deeper than words written centuries ago.

When Warrick kissed his bride, Amelia was vaguely aware of applause and whistles of approval. They quickly turned into ribald predictions that the endless kiss might set the church afire.

∼

Warrick would have preferred to take his bride straight to bed, but he'd never hear the end of it from Lady Penelope if he and Amelia didn't preside over the wedding breakfast.

The event proved to be entertaining. The guests were mostly family, their number supplemented by members of the Derbyshire gentry.

The women were fascinated by Lady Penelope's hat which she apparently felt obliged to explain was inspired by Marie Antoinette. Warrick visualized the ill-fated queen going to the guillotine with ostrich and peacock feathers stuck in her hair.

However, his mother-in-law was upstaged by Dorothea Derby Fortescue who stole hearts as Philip proudly carried his daughter around the ballroom for all to see. Warrick was rather pleased with Philip and

Jenny's decision to include the place of her birth in the babe's name.

"Mama won't be pleased," Amelia whispered close to his ear.

Warrick didn't care. If he sired a daughter he certainly didn't plan to name her Penelope. However, this wasn't the moment to voice that opinion. Instead, he squeezed his wife's hand already curled around his rampant arousal, hoping he could soon carry his bride to their bedchamber.

A BEDDING

Amelia was relieved when time finally came to leave the dining room with her husband, though she missed having Warrick's male heat in her hand.

"One detour, my love," she whispered as they climbed the stairs. "I promised Jenny."

Jaw clenched, he nodded.

She tapped lightly and Mrs. Brest ushered them into the chamber. "Doin' fine, she is, ducks. Not too long, mind."

Amelia smiled. She liked the Derbyshire habit of calling everyone a duck, but her smile soon fled.

Jenny sat propped up in bed, lines of fatigue marring her beauty. "Dotty has a fine pair of lungs," she explained. "Kept us up most of the night."

Warrick squeezed Amelia's hand, looking more uneasy than she'd ever seen him. Being in the bedchamber of a woman who'd recently delivered a baby apparently made a man nervous.

"We've come to show you our wedding finery," Amelia explained, kissing her sister's cheek.

"You both look wonderful," Jenny replied. "I'm sorry we can't leave right away so you can enjoy your honeymoon without having Fortescues underfoot."

Amelia controlled the urge to snort. The Duke and Duchess of Beaufort's idea of a honeymoon involved spending hours pleasuring each other in bed. "Nonsense," she replied. "Stay as long as you need to. You being here won't interfere with our plans at all."

∼

Warrick smiled at his bride as they walked down the landing to the master chamber. "You're a born diplomat," he said.

"My sister isn't fooled. She knows what we're about," she replied, squealing when her feet left the floor and he carried her across the threshold of his chamber.

It seemed he'd waited an eternity to make Amelia completely his. The instinct was to get naked as quickly as possible and do the deed.

However, a gentleman would exercise more finesse, beginning with a kiss.

She opened her mouth readily, teasing his tongue with her own. She seemed innocently reluctant to make things easy.

Restraint was going to require willpower. His throbbing cock scoffed at the notion.

It came to him she was trying to reach the laces behind her back, all the while suckling his tongue, letting him breathe for her. He came to her aid and the bodice sagged off her shoulders when he undid the ties. She pulled it down further to expose her breasts.

He filled his lungs, praying he wouldn't embarrass himself before he even got inside her. She moaned when he suckled a turgid nipple. Things were going from bad to worse.

Suddenly, their gazes met.

"Don't hold back on my account," she said. "I want you inside me, now."

Her confession resurrected the genuine Warrick.

He later wasn't sure how he managed to undress them both within a minute, but his happy cock didn't care as it slid into wet warmth. The tightness of her pulsating sheath only inflamed him more as he plunged in and out, in and out. She was screaming, digging her nails into his back, matching his frantic rhythm. He had to assume she was as enraptured as he was because he sure as hell couldn't stop now. He growled her name as he leaped into the abyss of blissful release.

∼

Still trying to count the thousands of stars behind her eyes, Amelia traced her fingertips through the sheen of sweat on Warrick's back.

"I'm too heavy," he muttered into her neck, though he made no effort to move.

How to tell him she relished his weight and had loved every moment of being the recipient of his unbridled passion? There'd been nothing genteel about their lovemaking. "You're mine now," she whispered, trusting he understood she loved the wild, earthy Warrick.

Or perhaps her cries of rapture had been enough.

"Forgive me," he said as his manhood left her body and curled up at her entry. "I should have tended to your pleasure but I couldn't wait."

"That you needed me so badly was exciting," she replied. "And I was ready."

"You were wet," he agreed.

She assumed the congress had been as good for him, but she would never ask.

"And tight," he added.

Was that a good thing?

He rolled off her and gathered her into his arms. "That was the best sex I've ever had," he confessed.

It was what she wanted to hear. Wasn't it?

～

WARRICK CURSED himself inwardly when Amelia stiffened in his embrace. Would he ever learn to think before he spoke? "I'm sorry. That didn't come out exactly as I intended."

"That's all right," she replied, softening a little. "I'm not naive enough to think I'm the first woman you've taken to your bed."

"But you're the only one I'll ever need, Amelia. The handful of others were about relieving male urges. You're about soaring to the heavens on a chariot of fire."

She put a hand on his chest, grazing his nipple with

her thumb. "I understand. When I felt your seed rush into my body..."

And that was all it took to get his cock's attention. He positioned her so he could suckle a nipple and let his fingers wander to stroke her nubbin. "Do you like that?" he asked when a moan emerged from deep in her throat.

"You know I do," she replied hoarsely.

When he dipped a finger into her wet warmth, she arched off the bed. He smothered her cries of ecstasy with his kiss, climbed atop her and positioned his cock at her entry. "Do you want more, little one?" he rasped.

"More, much more," she pleaded.

He was only too happy to oblige.

THE HUNTING LODGE

"It's been a revelation," Amelia confessed as she and Warrick waved until the Wentworth carriage was out of sight.

"Alone at last," he said, gathering her into his embrace.

It seemed taking care of newborn babies wasn't something her husband wanted to discuss. She'd had little to do with Sax when he was tiny and only minimal interaction with Avery and Rowland who were already toddlers. Two weeks of Dorothea Derby Fortescue's hungry screams in the middle of the night had been enough to try the patience of a saint. How Warrick and the lads had slept through it, she'd never know. They had explained that the wailing of infants was something you got used to in the slums. Still, she didn't want to harp on in case Warrick thought it had put her off having children. As Jenny kept saying, it was different when it was your own child.

"Seriously?" she replied to his comment, gesturing to

the boys who were headed back inside. "Alone? With those five in the house?"

"At least they don't expect to be fed in the middle of the night."

So, he wasn't deaf to a babe's cries, after all!

"Don't worry," he assured her, bestowing a kiss on the top of her head. "We'll manage when our turn comes."

"I know. You'll be an amazing father."

"Which brings me to my next question," he said.

"Which is?" she asked, curious about the hesitation in his voice.

"Our honeymoon. Er...I was thinking we'd enjoy a few days hiking the dales."

She understood immediately. "I'm sure the lads would love that."

"I'll make the arrangements," he replied with a relieved smile.

"It will be a wonderful learning opportunity for them," she said as they walked back to the house.

"Spoken like a true governess. But you must realize we'll have to find someone else to take on that role."

She'd known the time would come, but it was difficult to deal with the reality that a duchess couldn't be a governess. "I still want to be involved in their education."

"And mine, I hope," he replied.

"Of course, and you can teach me new ways to please you."

"Amelia," he breathed, pulling her into his arms. "Can we start now?"

Arrangements for the proposed hiking holiday fell into place once Warrick learned from Wilson that the dukedom owned a hunting lodge in the Peak District.

Summoned from Derby, an outfitter provided suitable footwear, clothing, knapsacks and walking sticks. He also gave them details of a local guide, should they require such services.

"Perhaps that's a good idea," Amelia remarked. "Until we get our bearings."

Warrick agreed. "It might prevent the lads from wandering off and getting lost."

Even as he spoke, he knew that was unlikely. His wards' behavior had improved greatly but they were adventurous boys who weren't afraid to tackle new challenges—perhaps a trait learned in the slums where harsh realities had to be faced head-on.

Amelia had never learned to ride. The outfitter informed them the carriage would take them as far as Buxton, from where they'd have to ride the rest of the way to the lodge. He undertook to arrange for the horses, and Amelia agreed to riding lessons.

Warrick had quickly acquired a love of horses when he'd first come to Cavendish. Watching his wife gradually lose her nervousness and settle into the saddle was a source of great pleasure. The horse soon knew who was in control.

Despite long nights of intense lovemaking, they fell into the habit of rising before dawn so they could enjoy an early morning ride together without the lads.

Amelia's apprehension grew as the carriage traveled closer to Buxton. The terrain was already hilly. For two weeks, she'd enjoyed learning to ride around the flat meadows around Cavendish Manor. Riding up hills and down dales would be a challenge. The boys were too quiet. Perhaps they were also worried.

"We'll take it slowly," Warrick said, obviously sensitive to her mood.

They stayed overnight in a comfortable inn in Buxton, emerging into the courtyard after a hearty breakfast. Amelia had envisaged herself riding a sleek, docile mare. What she got was a pony with a defiant glare in its eyes.

"This 'ere's Gertrude, ducks, er, I mean Yer Grace," the man hired as their guide explained. "She'll teck thee where ye wants to go."

Grinning broadly, Warrick helped her mount.

"What's funny?" she demanded, feeling uncharacteristically gauche.

"Nothing," he replied, mounting his own pony.

"I should be laughing at you," she countered. "Your legs are too long for that poor animal."

The guide led the way.

It quickly became apparent that Gertrude knew the narrow trail they followed. Any attempt to divert her from it was ignored. When they paused at a small lake to refresh the ponies, Gertrude marched resolutely into the water to drink, despite Amelia's frantic efforts to rein her in. She felt ridiculous sitting in the middle of the lake, subject to the whim of the shaggy beast. Warrick's grin didn't help matters.

When they resumed their journey, Amelia decided to relax and trust the pony. There really was no other choice. She lapsed into a doze, from which she was suddenly jolted by shouting.

Startled, she rubbed her eyes. "I must be dreaming," she said. "It's bigger than our old cottage in Beverley."

~

THE SIGHT of the hunting lodge, and the number of servants who emerged to greet them, brought home to Warrick how wide a gap existed between the aristocracy and ordinary people. How far removed *he* was from his roots. He'd imagined a rustic cabin, something akin to a shepherd's bothy, and worried about making love to Amelia with the boys at close quarters. "They could each have their own *fyking* room in this place," he muttered.

As he might have expected, the lads had already dismounted and rushed off to explore their holiday digs. He realized Amelia was still mounted, looking at him expectantly.

"It's bigger than I thought," she said after he slid off his pony and helped her down.

"That's an understatement," he replied.

"We're going to have a marvelous time here," she declared, smiling broadly.

Her happiness forced him out of his sour mood. She was right. There was nothing to be gained by denying he was wealthy, no point in not enjoying the fruits of his good fortune. The lads certainly deserved this experience, as did he and Amelia.

"You know," she said, pausing in the entryway lined with a display of hundreds of deer antlers and one particularly intimidating boar's head. "It occurs to me this place could well serve as an adjunct to the school we're planning. Sort of an outdoor learning experience."

If he'd ever had doubts he could succeed as a duke, his duchess swept them away like chaff on the wind.

EPILOGUE
FIVE YEARS LATER

"She was sometimes a difficult person to live with," Eliza said hoarsely. "But we'll miss her."

Amelia stared at the simple headstone in the cemetery behind Beverley Minster. "Two Saxtons now. Papa and his Penelope reunited."

"When we knew she hadn't long to live, Alex generously offered a plot in the Harrowby family cemetery on the estate," Eliza said. "Surprisingly, she wouldn't hear of it."

Holding hands, the sisters stood for long minutes, each lost in memories of their extraordinary mother.

"We'd better show our faces at the wake," Jenny finally said. "Mama wouldn't approve of us arriving late."

They walked to the ancient church and descended the stone steps to the undercroft.

The murmur of conversation ceased as soon as they were noticed. It unsettled Amelia. She wanted to insist the several dozen mourners go back to consuming the plates full of crustless sandwiches and *petits fours* prepared by the kitchen staff at Harrowby Hall.

Warrick took her elbow. "They want to pay their respects," he said softly, making her aware people were on the move.

"Good grief," she exclaimed as Alex organized the members of her family. "Even our children?"

She'd wager the Minster had rarely seen such a receiving line. Three dukes, three duchesses and eight noble progeny. "Mama would be proud," she whispered, swallowing the lump in her throat.

As the eldest boy and heir to a dukedom, Sax could be expected to perform solidly, but Amelia doubted her four-year-old twins would stay the course. Broxton and Beverly never kept still for long. She'd give them five minutes. Then, her son would pull his sister's braid and all hell would break loose when she retaliated.

However, nannies were keeping a sharp eye and would corral any wayward offspring.

Most of the well-wishers were strangers to Amelia, but their condolences seemed genuine. With sentiments like *soul of discretion* and *patience of a saint*, she wondered if some of them had ever actually met Lady Penelope Saxton.

She was, however, glad to see Kenneth Watkins who'd been a tutor at the Saxton Academy for nearly a year. She'd proposed the name for the school, thrilled when it was agreed upon. Her intention was not to honor her mother, as Eliza and Jenny both understood, but their long dead father. He'd mishandled his family's finances with catastrophic results, but he'd been determined his girls should have a good education. Thanks to him, his daughters had all married well.

With Kenneth came a broad-shouldered Eddie Powell, recently appointed to manage the Saxton Academy's Wilderness School in the Peak District. "Have you heard from Tim and Tom?" she asked.

"No, Your Grace," he replied. "I expect it takes a while for letters to arrive from Upper Canada."

"Yes," she agreed. "And I have no idea where Fort William is. A fur trading outpost in the middle of nowhere, I'm told."

She'd been as surprised as anyone when the timid twosome had suddenly turned adventurous and signed on as clerks with the Northwest Company.

A dapper Charlie Hart appeared a few minutes later. Warrick had taken him on as his valet when Carlos decided to return to Spain.

"Happy?" Warrick asked when the last person had filed through the line.

"It's a wake," she retorted with a smile, knowing full well what he meant. "I'm not supposed to be happy."

"Fine young gentlemen, our wards," he said proudly.

"Thanks to you. And soon there'll be more. The first group of pupils matriculates this year. Michael and Peter have already secured employment. Since William and Josiah Mawdsley passed on, Archibald needs more clerks to help him."

"Excellent," he replied.

"Which reminds me, I think girls should have the opportunity to attend the school. I intend to speak to the Chairman of the Board of Governors about it."

"Er..this year, that would be me, darling."

"Exactly. Shall we say later tonight? I'd better go speak to our daughter about kicking people, or your heir might be permanently unmanned."

"Minx," he replied.

THE END

Wondering what happened to Alexander Harcourt at Waterloo that made him The Unkissable Duke?

Waterloo, June 18th, 1815

Across from the Brussels Road near Waterloo, Colonel Alexander Harcourt shifted his weight in Diablo's saddle as he inspected his regiment. A persistent feeling of impending doom lay heavily on his shoulders. His men stood like toy soldiers as they watched Napoleon's massive army take up positions on the opposite slopes of the escarpment. His favorite warhorse snorted and tossed his head. Ashen faces and sternly set jaws confirmed the gut-wrenching fear gnawing at every man's innards. He hoped his earlier speech about courage and perseverance had bolstered their determination to emerge victorious.

The crack of a rifle shot broke the eerie silence and produced a ripple of surprised gasps among the troops. It briefly occurred to him the sound was strangely close. There was no opportunity to ponder the matter further when Diablo reared, screeching as he staggered. Heart surging into his throat, Alex tried frantically to disentangle his booted feet from the stirrups and leap free of the terrified beast as it collapsed into the mud. He had a fleeting impression of shock on the faces of his men before he was struck hard in the face as he hit the ground. As pain exploded in one eye, the ridiculous thought crossed his mind that he'd be upset if his nose was broken. An enormous weight sent the air whooshing from his lungs and shattered more than his nose. Gagging on the overwhelming horror of his beloved Diablo's dying agony, what little remained of his wits told him he was dead before the battle even began.

Grab UNKISSABLE DUKE now.

ANNA'S STORY

As an amateur genealogist (aka an addict of family tree research) I became obsessed with tracing my English roots back to the Norman Conquest in the 11th century.

This turned out to be a pipe dream since I am not descended from the nobility and records were not kept for "common folks" until much later. Even then, early parish records are often indecipherable.

As a result, I began to write stories about a noble medieval family I conjured from my imagination. The Montbryces were born.

Like many people, I had an inner compulsion to write one good book. What was originally intended as that one book about my fictional family eventually became the 12-book series, The Montbryce Legacy.

In other words, writing superseded genealogy as my principal addiction, and I have since published more than 60 novels and novellas. Almost all are historical romances that feature Vikings, Highlanders, medieval knights, Elizabethan goldsmiths or Regency aristocrats. You can find more details on my website https://annamarkland.com/.

I've lived most of my life in Canada, though I was born in the UK. An English grammar school education instilled in me a love of European history which continues to this day. While I may boast of being a proud Canadian, I'm still a Lancashire lass at heart.

Before becoming a full-time writer, I was an elementary school teacher, a job I loved. I then worked as administrator for a world-wide disaster relief organization.

I love cats, although I haven't been able to bring myself to adopt another one since unexpectedly losing Topaz a few years ago.

I have few domestic skills. You'll notice most of my heroines hate sewing!

I try to follow three simple writing guidelines. I give my characters free rein to tell their story, which often turns out to be different from the original version in my head. I'm a firm believer in love at first sight. My protagonists may initially deny the attraction but, eventually, my heroes and heroines find their soul mates. It seems only natural then to include scenes of intimacy enjoyed by people who love each other deeply. I believe such intimacy is wholesome. Historical accuracy is important to me, although I have been known to tweak history when necessary. I write romance because I find happy endings very satisfying.

You can find me on all the usual social media platforms. On Facebook as Anna Markland and Anna Markland Novels, on Instagram as annamarkland, and Pinterest and BookBub as Anna Markland. I also have a reader group on Facebook called Markland's Merrymakers and new members are always welcome.

For their help in polishing this manuscript, I'd like to acknowledge the assistance of Sylvie Grayson, Jacquie Biggar, Reggi Allder, LizAnn Carson, Alison Pridie and Maria McIntyre.

Printed in Great Britain
by Amazon